Praise for the Chocoholic Mysteries

The Chocolate Frog Frame-Up

"A JoAnna Carl mystery will be a winner. The trivia and vivid descriptions of the luscious confections are enough to make you hunger for more!"
—Roundtable Reviews

"Delicious." —Cluesunlimited

"A fast-paced, light read, full of chocolate facts and delectable treats. Lee is an endearing heroine. . . . Readers will enjoy the time they spend with Lee and Joe in Warner Pier and will look forward to returning for more murder dipped in chocolate."
—The Mystery Reader

"The descriptions of the chocolates are enough to make your mouth water, so be prepared. . . . Once again, I enjoyed each page of the book and am already looking forward to my next visit to Warner Pier, Michigan." —Review Index

continued . . .

The Chocolate Bear Burglary

"Do not read *The Chocolate Bear Burglary* on an empty stomach because the luscious . . . descriptions of exotic chocolate will have you running out to buy gourmet sweets . . . a delectable treat." —*Midwest Book Review*

"[Carl] teases with descriptions of mouthwatering bonbons and truffles while she drops clues. . . . [Lee is] vulnerable and real, endearingly defective. . . . Fast-paced and sprinkled with humor. Strongly recommended." —*I Love a Mystery*

"Kept me entertained to the very last word . . . a great new sleuth. . . . Interesting facts about chocolate. . . . a delicious new series." —*Romantic Times*

The Chocolate Cat Caper

"A mouthwatering debut and a delicious new series! Feisty young heroine Lee McKinney is a delight in this chocolate treat. A real page-turner, and I got chocolate on every one! I can't wait for the next."

—Tamar Myers

"As delectable as a rich chocolate truffle and the mystery filling satisfies to the last prized morsel. Lee McKinney sells chocolates and solves crimes with panache and good humor. More, please. And I'll take one of those dark chocolate oval bonbons. . . ."

—Carolyn Hart

"One will gain weight just from reading [this]. . . . Delicious . . . the beginning of what looks like a terrific new cozy series." —*Midwest Book Review*

"Enjoyable . . . entertaining . . . a fast-paced whodunit with lots of suspects and plenty of surprises . . . satisfies a passion for anything chocolate. In the fine tradition of Diane Mott Davidson."

—*The Commercial Record* (MI)

Also by JoAnna Carl

The Chocolate Cat Caper
The Chocolate Bear Burglary
The Chocolate Frog Frame-Up
The Chocolate Puppy Puzzle

The Chocolate Mouse Trap

A Chocoholic Mystery

JoAnna Carl

A SIGNET BOOK

SIGNET
Published by New American Library, a division of
Penguin Group (USA) Inc., 375 Hudson Street,
New York, New York 10014, USA
Penguin Group (Canada), 90 Eglinton Avenue East, Suite 700, Toronto,
Ontario M4P 2Y3, Canada (a division of Pearson Penguin Canada Inc.)
Penguin Books Ltd., 80 Strand, London WC2R 0RL, England
Penguin Ireland, 25 St. Stephen's Green, Dublin 2,
Ireland (a division of Penguin Books Ltd.)
Penguin Group (Australia), 250 Camberwell Road, Camberwell, Victoria 3124,
Australia (a division of Pearson Australia Group Pty. Ltd.)
Penguin Books India Pvt. Ltd., 11 Community Centre, Panchsheel Park,
New Delhi - 110 017, India
Penguin Group (NZ), cnr Airborne and Rosedale Roads, Albany,
Auckland 1310, New Zealand (a division of Pearson New Zealand Ltd.)
Penguin Books (South Africa) (Pty.) Ltd., 24 Sturdee Avenue,
Rosebank, Johannesburg 2196, South Africa

Penguin Books Ltd., Registered Offices:
80 Strand, London WC2R 0RL, England

First published by Signet, an imprint of New American Library,
a division of Penguin Group (USA) Inc.

First Printing, September 2005
10 9 8 7

To Dave,
still my special guy

Acknowledgments

As ever, I owe many thanks to Morgen Chocolate in Dallas and the great staff there—especially my daughter, Betsy Peters. I also received help from Michigan friends and neighbors Susan McDermott, Tracy Paquin, and Bonnie Miller. Computer advice came from Joe Diaz and John Hornbeck, and literary information came from Dr. John Morris.

Chapter 1

"I'm sick and tired of killing this stupid inspirational junk," I said. "If Julie Singletree doesn't stop sending it, I'm going to kill her, as well as her messages."

I'd been talking to myself, but when I raised my eyes from the computer screen, I realized I was also snarling at Aunt Nettie. She had nothing to do with the e-mail that had been driving me crazy, but she had innocently walked into my office, making herself a handy target for a glare.

Aunt Nettie smiled placidly; she'd understood that I was mad at my e-mail, not her. "Are you talking about that silly girl who's trying to be a party planner?"

"Yes. I know she got us that big order for the chocolate mice, but I'm beginning to think the business she could throw our way can't be worth the nausea brought on by these daily doses of Victorian sentiment."

Aunt Nettie settled her solid Dutch figure into a chair and adjusted the white food-service hairnet that covered her hair—blond, streaked with gray. I don't know how she works with chocolate all day long and keeps her white tunic and pants so sparkling clean.

"Victorian sentiment isn't your style, Lee," she said.

"Julie is sending six of us half a dozen messages every day, and I am not interested in her childish view of life. She alternates between ain't-life-grand and ain't-life-a-bitch, but both versions are coated with silly sugar. She never has anything clever or witty. Just dumb."

"Why haven't you asked to be taken off her list?"

I sighed and reached into my top desk drawer to raid my stash for a Bailey's Irish Cream bonbon ("Classic cream liqueur interior in dark chocolate"). I'd worked for TenHuis Chocolade for more than two years, but I wasn't at all tired of our products, described on our stationery as "Handmade chocolates in the Dutch tradition." When you're hassled by minor annoyances, such as e-mail, nothing soothes the troubled mind like a dose of chocolate.

Aunt Nettie was waiting for an answer, and I was hard put to find one. "I suppose I kept thinking that if I didn't respond she'd simply drop me from her jokes and junk list," I said.

"You didn't even want to tell her you don't want to receive any more spam?"

"Oh, it's not spam. She's made up a little list of us—it's all west Michigan people connected with the fine foods and parties trade. Lindy's on it, thanks to her new job in catering. There's Jason Foster—you know, he's got the contract for the new restaurant at Warner Point. There's Carolyn Rose, at House of Roses—she carries a line of gourmet items. Margaret Van Meter from Holland—the cake decorating gal. And the Denhams, at Hideaway Inn. We're all on the list. And since we all deal in fancy foods, Julie has named us the 'Seventh Major Food Group.' You know—grains, dairy, vegetables, fruit, meat, fats, and party food."

"It *is* a funny name."

"It's the only witty idea Julie ever had." I gestured toward the screen. "This message is typical. 'A Prayer for the Working Woman.' I haven't read it, but I already know what it says."

"What?" Aunt Nettie smiled. "Since I've worked all my life, I might benefit from a little prayer."

"I can make you a printout, if you can stand the grossly lush roses Julie uses as a border." I punched the appropriate keys as I talked. "I predict it will be about how downtrodden women are today because most of us work."

"Since I own my own business, I guess I'm one of the downtrodders, not the downtrodden."

"Exactly!" I spoke before I thought, but luckily my reaction amused Aunt Nettie. We both laughed. Then I began to backpedal. "You're a dream to work for, Aunt Nettie. You're definitely not a downtrodder. And you're not downtrodden, because you enjoy your job. But Julie can't seem to make up her mind. If she isn't sending stuff claiming today's women are put-upon because we have to work, she's sending stuff saying we don't get a chance at the good jobs. I can understand both views, but she wraps them up in enough syrup to make a hundred maple cream truffles."

"You'll have to assert yourself, Lee. Tell her you don't like her e-mails."

I sighed. "About the time I tell her that, she'll actually land a big wedding, and the bride will want enough bonbons and truffles for four hundred people, and we'll lose out on a couple of thousand dollars in business. Or Schrader Laboratories will plan another banquet and want an additional three hundred souvenir boxes of mice."

I gestured toward the decorated gift box on the corner of my desk. Aunt Nettie had shipped off the order two weeks before, but I'd saved one as a sample. The box contained a dozen one-inch chocolate mice—six replicas of laboratory mice in white chocolate and six tiny versions of a computer mouse, half in milk chocolate and half in dark.

Schrader Laboratories is a Grand Rapids firm that does product testing—sometimes using laboratory mice and sometimes computers. A special item like the souvenir made for their annual dinner means risk-free profit for TenHuis Chocolade; we know they're sold before we order the boxes they'll be packed in.

"That was a nice bit of business Julie threw our way, even if she did get the order from a relative," I said. "I can put up with a certain amount of gooey sentiment for that amount of money."

"It might be cheaper to give it up than to hire a psychiatrist. You've got plenty to do. Tell Julie your mean old boss has cracked down on nonbusiness e-mail."

Aunt Nettie smiled her usual sweet smile. "And I really am going to add to your chores. We need Amaretto."

"I'll get some on my way home."

Amaretto is used to flavor a truffle that is extremely popular with TenHuis Chocolade customers. Our product list describes it as "Milk chocolate interior flavored with almond liqueur and coated in white chocolate." The truffle is decorated with three milk chocolate stripes, but its mainly white color makes it an ideal accent for boxes of Valentine candy and at that moment we were just four weeks away from Valentine's Day. I knew Aunt Nettie and the twenty-five ladies who actually make TenHuis chocolates had been using a lot of Amaretto as they got ready for the major chocolate holiday. But liqueurs go a long way when used only for flavoring; one bottle would probably see us through the rush.

I handed Aunt Nettie the printout of Julie's dumb e-mail—all ten pages of it. Julie never cleans the previous messages off the bottom of e-mails she forwards or replies to. Then Aunt Nettie went back to her antiseptically clean workroom.

I wrote "Amaretto" on a Post-it and stuck the note to the side of my handbag before I turned back to my computer. I manipulated my mouse until the arrow was on REPLY ALL and clicked it. Then I stared at the screen, trying to figure out how to be tactful and still stop Julie's daily drivel.

"Dear Seventh Major Food Group," I typed. Maybe Julie wouldn't feel that I'd singled her out. "This is one of the busiest seasons for the chocolate business, and my aunt and I have decided we simply have to crack down on nonbusiness e-mail. At least half our orders come in by e-mail, so I spend a lot of time clearing it. As great as the jokes and inspirational material that we exchange on this list can be," I lied, "I just can't justify the time I spend reading them. So please drop me from the joke/inspiration list. But please continue to include me in the business tips!"

I sent the message to the whole list, feeling smug. I was genuinely hopeful that I'd managed to drop the cornball philosophy without dropping some valuable business associates along with it.

I wasn't prepared the next day when I got a call from Lindy Herrera, my best friend and a manager for Herrera Catering.

"Lee!" Lindy sounded frantic. "Have you had the television on?"

"No. Why?"

"I was watching the news on the Grand Rapids station. Oh, Lee, it's awful!"

"What's happened?"

"It's Julie Singletree! She's been murdered!"

Chapter 2

I hadn't known Julie well.

Lindy and I had met her two months earlier at the West Michigan Bridal Fair, a big-time event held in Grand Rapids. I'd gone to the fair for both professional and personal reasons.

On the professional side, as business manager of TenHuis Chocolade, located in the Lake Michigan resort town of Warner Pier, I'm responsible for marketing. I also keep the books, write the salary checks, send out the statements, and pay the taxes. As one part of its business, TenHuis Chocolade provides arrays of truffles, bonbons, and molded chocolates for special occasions—occasions which have been known to include wedding receptions. We also make specialty items—tiny chocolate champagne bottles, chocolate roses, molded chocolate gift boxes with names on top, and dozens of other chocolate objects—which would be suitable for weddings. Visiting a bridal fair would be a good way to make some contacts that could possibly lead to sales.

On the personal side, I was planning my own wedding, and it wasn't proving to be an easy job.

For nearly two years I'd been dating Joe Woodyard, a Warner Pier native who earns his living by an unlikely combination of careers. He's an expert in restoring antique wooden boats and is also city attorney for the town of Warner Pier, Michigan (pop. 2,503). We'd both had unhappy first marriages, so it had taken us—or at least me—quite a while to decide to head for the altar a second time.

This time, we both vowed, we were going to do it "right." As if there's a foolproof way to get married. The problem was that Joe's version of "right" didn't mesh with mine.

Early on Joe and I had discovered that we'd both flown to Las Vegas to get married the first time around. That more or less ruled out a romantic elopement. Been there, done that.

So Joe asked if I wanted to go back to my Texas hometown for the ceremony.

I laughed harshly. "Then I'd have to invite my parents."

"You don't want to invite your parents?"

"Not both of them. But it's fine if your mom wants to be there."

"Now wait a moment, Lee. You don't want either of your parents to come to our wedding?"

"My dad would be okay. He's helped me out a lot. But he'd have to bring my stepmother. And if she's there, my mom would go bananas. So it's just better not to get into it. Can't we just have Aunt Nettie? And Lindy and Tony and your mom—and Mike, if you want to. And maybe Hogan Jones."

Mike Herrera is my friend Lindy's father-in-law and boss—and he dates Joe's mother. And Hogan Jones is Warner Pier police chief, and he's been taking my Aunt Nettie out. Small towns are like that: interconnected.

Joe was frowning. "Don't you think your mom will be upset if you don't ask her to the wedding and do ask your aunt?"

I thought about it a moment. "Frankly, Joe, I don't care if my mother is upset, as long as she's upset in Dallas, not in Warner Pier. She hasn't exactly been supportive of me and my needs and desires. If she had her way, I'd still be married to Rich. I'm sorry, but I'm not on good terms with my mother or my stepmother. It would really complicate matters if I tried to have them at the wedding."

Joe's frown deepened. "Then the wedding will have to be really small."

"Does that bother you?"

"I admit I'd put the money from selling the Chris-Craft Utility aside to pay for a big blowout. I thought you might want to get married in Texas, then have a reception up here."

That pretty much stopped the discussion. Obviously Joe did want to have a biggish wedding. I didn't. Right at the moment I didn't see any chance of compromise. A big wedding would involve my parents, and no miracle was likely to make me friends with both of them at this late date.

But when I went up to DeVos Place, the Grand Rapids convention center, for the West Michigan Bridal Fair, maybe I was looking for some solution to our problem, some way to have a big wedding for Joe and a little one for me. Some way to involve my parents in the whole event and not cause an open split.

The convention center was a madhouse, of course. The brides and the bridegrooms looked either frantic or confused, and the mothers were terrifying. And that was just the parking lot. I paid my admission, but I was almost afraid to go in the door. The inside was likely to be even worse.

And it was. It was a hubbub of music, talking,

arguing. ("I'm *not* wearing Aunt Emma's stupid mantilla, Mother! It makes me look like a Spanish tart.") Lace, satin, sequins, embossed napkins, multitiered cakes, crystal punch bowls, silver candelabra, wrought-iron arches, exotic flowers—for a moment I was definitely sorry I'd come. But I took a deep breath, shouldered my tote bag and started working the crowd. Up one aisle and down the next, picking out the caterers and wedding planners, asking to speak to the person in charge of the booth, giving a brief pitch on chocolate, and thrusting a brochure at them. In there somewhere I usually managed to mention my own wedding; that got their attention faster than the TenHuis brochure.

By the end of the second aisle I was glad I'd had the sense to wear flat heels. That's when I heard someone call my name. "Lee! Lee McKinney! Over here!"

I turned around and saw a booth with an arch that read, HERRERA CATERING—THE COMPLETE PARTY PROVIDER. And under the arch was a friendly face. "Lindy!"

Lindy and I have been friends since we worked at TenHuis Chocolade together the year we were both sixteen. She still has the same dimpled smile that made her the prettiest girl on Warner Pier Beach. She's a little plumper now, after having three kids, and she's recently had her brown hair cut into a sophisticated bob.

"Come over here and sit down," Lindy said. "You look as confused as the rest of these brides."

"I guess TenHuis should have taken a booth. But that's expensive."

"It would be a waste of money, since weddings aren't your main business. I can hand out some of your brochures."

"Thanks. Are you going to be able to get away for lunch?"

"Sure. I brought Delia—Mike's secretary. She's at lunch now. I never come to these without a partner to act as backup for when I need to hit the ladies room."

"Smart idea."

"I told Jason Foster we'd go to lunch with him. Do you remember Jason? He was a bartender for Mike for five years."

Mike, Lindy's father-in-law, is officially Miguel Herrera. He owns three restaurants in Warner Pier, plus the catering service. He employs a lot of people, both full and part-time, but Jason stood out.

"I'll never forget Jason," I said. "He and I were tending bar the night . . ." My voice failed me, but Lindy nodded. She had also been working the big party when Clementine Ripley bit into an Amaretto truffle and dropped dead. A lot of people remembered that night.

"Does Jason still wear his hair in a queue like George Washington?" I asked.

"Yep. And his forehead is higher than ever, so it still looks as if all his hair slid backward. And you know what Jason is up to now."

I grinned. "Well, I did hear that he had the contract to operate the new restaurant at Warner Point."

"Right. Mike was dying to take it on, but, of course he can't do that and be mayor, too. Just a little conflict of interest. I guess Joe told you all about it."

"All Joe told me is that he was signing the property over and leaving its operation up to the city."

Warner Point is a Warner Pier landmark, of sorts. The property formerly belonged to Joe's first—and ex—wife, Clementine Ripley. Ms. Ripley, who had a national reputation as a defense attorney, had died there two years earlier, leaving her legal affairs in a mess after eating the previously mentioned Amaretto truffle. Not only was the property heavily mortgaged, but she had also failed to make a new will after she and Joe were divorced. Under the old one, he inherited. This had been a personal problem for me, because the guy I was falling in love with had had to spend more than a year concentrating on the business affairs of his ex-wife. Neither of us found this romantic.

To add to the confusion, Joe had been determined not to benefit financially from the situation, beyond being reimbursed for his personal expenses. It had taken him a long time, but he had recently managed to turn the property—including its showpiece mansion—over to the City of Warner Pier. Mike Herrera and the city council wanted to develop it as a conference center, and Jason Foster had signed a contract to operate the restaurant and catering facility.

Lindy nodded. "Jason's trying to drum up some wedding receptions for the new restaurant."

"A competitor for Herrera Catering?"

"Not really. We cooperate, share employees and equipment. He's going to introduce me to a wedding planner at lunch. I thought you might like to meet her, too."

So that's how I met Julie Singletree. Jason, Lindy, and I walked over to the luxury hotel adjoining the Convention Center and went into the restaurant that overlooks the river. Julie impressed me immediately. Not only had she snagged a large table with a prize view; she was the cutest little thing in the place.

Julie's short black hair was perfect, her black eyes snapped, and her black suit fit like a million dollars, which was probably what she paid for it. She was the very picture of an up-and-coming professional woman. A miniature professional woman. That suit couldn't have been any bigger than size 3, and even in three-inch heels, Julie barely reached my shoulder.

I am, after all, close to six feet tall—nearly a foot taller than Julie. It also occurred to me that I was older than Julie. I was about to turn thirty, and Julie looked as if she were barely old enough to sign the tab for enough champagne for a wedding reception. And I was also dowdier than Julie, even in my good navy blazer. Before she could make me feel inferior, I straightened my shoulders and reminded myself that I'm a natural blond. That's not unusual in western Michigan, but it counts for something.

Her business, Julie told us, was just getting started. "My grandmother gave me an *advance* on my inheritance. She's a *sweetheart*! I'd just feel *awful* if I wasted her money!"

Then she waved her hand casually. "I ran into some more *Warner Pier* people over at the show. So I invited them to *join* us. I hope you don't *mind*. My grandmother has a *cottage* down there, and I always spent the summer there when I was a kid. I simply *adore* Warner Pier, so I hope I can *capture* all the business down that way."

"Who is your grandmother?" Lindy asked the question faster than I could. Somehow I wasn't surprised when Julie blushed slightly and said her grandmother was Rachel Schrader. The name made it plain that Julie's grandmother could afford to give her granddaughter an advance on her inheritance.

Mrs. Schrader was well known as a west Michigan philanthropist, and her Warner Pier "cottage" was no little weekend cabin. It was a mansion sitting on more than a hundred acres of lakeshore property. Lindy, Jason, and I were careful not to meet each other's eyes.

Julie went on talking, verbally italicizing at least one word in every sentence. And in a few minutes, Warner Pier people wandered in and began to join us. Of course, Lindy and I already knew all of them. Warner Pier merchants can hardly avoid getting acquainted with each other. There aren't that many of us.

Ronnie and Diane Denham came next. They own the Hideaway Inn. Ronnie's a retired engineer, so he handles the maintenance for their bed-and-breakfast. Diane had been a teacher, but her avocation is cooking. She specializes in fancy breakfasts. They told us they'd decided to advertise the Hideaway as a honeymoon destination.

Both Ronnie and Diane have wavy white hair, the kind with great body. Both have bright blue eyes, and both are on the plump side. They've always reminded me of Mr. and Mrs. Santa Claus.

As Julie greeted them, I remember wondering if Joe and I would look that much alike after thirty years of marriage. Joe and I are both tall, bony people, and if his dark hair turned gray and my blond hair did, too . . . It was a frightening idea. But I thought his eyes would stay blue and mine hazel.

Carolyn Rose came clomping in. Her high-heeled boots were audible clear across the restaurant, and almost immediately I heard her low, throaty voice. "I hope this place has decent coffee." She didn't greet anybody; just yanked out a chair and threw herself into it, tossing her fake fur jacket over the back and running her fingers through her unnaturally bright red hair. "I had to get the flowers to the Huizenga funeral before I could leave Warner Pier. Somehow my usual dose of caffeine got lost in transit."

Like many Warner Pier retailers, Carolyn kept her shop open only a few hours a week in the winter—our off-season. She had no winter employees; so I knew she'd had to make up the sprays and wreaths, then take them to the funeral home herself, unload them, and help the funeral home people arrange them for the service.

Jason stood up to look for a waitress. His appearance seemed to draw the attention of a woman who had been hesitating at the door. She waved at our table enthusiastically, then walked over to us, smiling broadly. "Hello, Julie! Greetings all! I'm Margaret Van Meter."

She plunked herself down in the last chair at our table as if her name were so famous we'd all know who she was. When I glanced at Lindy, however, she looked as blank as I felt.

Julie gestured. "Margaret's a *baker*," she said. "She makes the most *fabulous* wedding cakes."

Margaret produced a handful of photographs of cakes and began handing them around. Or maybe "photographs" was too fancy a name for what Margaret had. "Snapshots" would have been more accurate. They were out of focus, with busy backgrounds. Some of the wedding cakes seemed to be tilting as if the bride and groom were planning to honeymoon in Italy and had been trying to get in the mood for a weekend in Pisa.

Margaret herself matched the photos: her mousy hair was straggly; her makeup was nonexistent; she was wearing jeans and a sweatshirt. She looked as if she'd gotten ready in the dark.

But the cakes in the photos—once you allowed for the amateur photography—were gorgeous.

Margaret began talking as emphatically as Julie had been. "No, I never use mixes," she told Diane Denham. "And I offer twenty flavors of fillings. Ooops!" She reached over and retrieved one of the photos. "How did that one get in there?"

"It looks interesting," Lindy said. "Is that your family?"

"The whole crew."

Margaret let Lindy have the photo, and I looked over her shoulder to see it. Margaret wasn't in it, but everybody else seemed to be. There were kids of every age up to eight or so—I counted six of them, including a small baby. They were grouped around a husky blond guy.

"You see why I can't get out to take a job," Margaret said. "I'm hoping I can earn some money at home."

Lindy produced a snapshot of the three Herrera kids, and we all seemed to forget we didn't know each other very well. It turned out to be a highly successful lunch, if you judge by the amount of laughing and funny stories. Jason's tale about the political candidate who was falling down drunk at a campaign banquet—well, I'd better not name names, but it was hilarious.

Of course, the Warner Pier crowd brought up my engagement.

"Oh!" Julie gave a squeal. "I *hope* you need a wedding planner."

"I'm sorry, Julie. I don't think we could justify a wedding planner. We're still discussing, but right now we're not planning for anything major. Lindy and her husband are going to be the only attendants."

"No *reception*?"

"We don't know yet."

"No cake?" Margaret sounded plaintive.

"Maybe. We haven't decided." Actually, I had been thinking one of Margaret's cakes might be just right, even if it had to be the smallest size.

"But you'll definitely need a romantic place to spend the wedding night." Ronnie Denham waggled his white eyebrows and grinned.

"This is the sexy go-round for both of us," I said. "So maybe we do need to emphasize romaine."

That stopped the conversation. I'd gotten my tongue completely twisted—a situation I'm sorry to say isn't all that uncommon.

I would have corrected my idiotic remark—"This is the second go-round for both of us. So maybe we do need to emphasize romance." But Lindy began to laugh.

Everyone joined in, even me. I've had to learn to laugh at my malapropisms. Or else I'd cry.

Lindy spoke again. "Sometimes Lee hides the fact that she's one of the smartest people in Warner Pier. And now maybe I'd better get back to the show."

"No, *no!*" Julie wasn't having it. "Not until we exchange cards!"

So we all brought out business cards—Margaret didn't have cards, so Lindy lent her some and she wrote her name, address, phone, and e-mail on the backs. The next day we all had an e-mail from Julie, telling us how *fantastically superwonderful* the luncheon had been and urging us all to stay in touch. That was when she declared us the "Seventh Major Food Group."

"Party food needs to be recognized," she wrote. "Maybe we'll start a movement. Grains, veggies, fruit, meats, dairy, fats/sugars are joined by PARTY!"

Her idea had seemed harmless enough, even though Julie had later turned out to be an annoying correspondent. I'd only seen her a few other times. She'd show up in Warner Pier without warning and ask if Lindy and I could go to lunch. The table talk was always about Lindy, me, or some of the other Seventh Food Group members. Julie never talked about herself, but she was always urging others to bare their souls. I didn't know her well enough to bare mine, so she and I hadn't become close friends.

Still, I wasn't prepared for the news that Julie had been murdered. It made me feel bad about sending her that e-mail asking her to drop the cornball sentiment. But I didn't feel guilty.

After all, there wasn't any connection between Julie's death and her e-mail.

Chapter 3

The e-mails flew furiously over the next few days,
as the Seventh Major Food Group exchanged information, shocked reactions, and gossip about Julie's death.

From the television and newspaper reports we
learned that the circumstances were mysterious, or
at least that the police weren't revealing much. Julie's
body had been discovered by an uncle, Martin
Schrader, who had gone by her apartment to take
her to lunch. The lunch date had been planned the
day before, but when Uncle Martin knocked, Julie
didn't answer her door. Her SUV was in the parking
lot. Uncle Martin got nervous and contacted the
apartment manager. Reading between the lines of the
news reports, I deduced that Uncle Martin had had
to do some arm twisting before the manager would
let him in. When the door was finally opened, Julie's
body had been in plain sight, lying in the living
room. The police said she had apparently died sometime the previous evening.

The police were cagey about the cause of death,
saying they'd wait for the results of the autopsy. But

I quizzed the Warner Pier police chief, Hogan Jones—who just happens to be a special friend of Aunt Nettie's. Hogan in turn quizzed some buddy he had on the Holland police force, and I learned that Julie's neck had been broken. There was no sign that she'd been sexually assaulted, or so Hogan's pal said.

Julie had lived in what we Texans call a "garden apartment," with a set of sliding doors that led to a private patio and deck. The deck door, Hogan found out, had been jimmied, and the police believed the killer got in that way.

Julie's apartment was in a complex just off U.S. Highway 31, one of Holland's major arteries. She had run her party and wedding planning business out of her apartment. The complex was fairly large, so there was lots of coming and going in its parking lot. That, added to the noise from the heavy traffic on the highway, meant that no one had noticed any strange activity around Julie's apartment. There was snow on the ground, but if any helpful footprints or tire tracks had been found, the police weren't saying anything about them, and Hogan's informant didn't volunteer any information Hogan wanted to share with me.

The Food Group members were all aghast, but each was aghast in a different way. "Oh, these girls today!" Diane Denham wrote. "They are so trusting. They meet people and invite them home when they know nothing about them, or about their families. They're so foolish." She was ignoring the evidence of the break-in, apparently. Ronnie usually left all the e-mail to her, so we didn't know what he thought.

Carolyn Rose represented the florists of the world. "I see the family is planning to designate memorial contributions to the Lake Michigan Conservation Society," she wrote. "Well, whatever floats their boat. Julie may have been Little Miss Knows-All, but she loved flowers. I'm planting a bed in the Dock Street Park in her memory. When I get time."

Having delivered the florist's credo, she had a few words to say about Julie. "Poor kid. It seems like a girl could have a little fun without getting murdered."

Jason singled out the killer for his remarks. "It must have been a madman," he wrote. "Julie could be thoughtless, but only a crazy person would have wanted to hurt her."

Margaret really seemed the most saddened. "I just loved Julie," she said. "She actually used to come by my house and bring lunch for me and the kids. She loved playing with them. She brought them wonderful presents. She was lonely. Now she'll never find the one person God meant for her."

Lindy's comments also reflected her own concerns. "Did Julie have an alarm system? Did she have Mace on her key chain? It can be scary, coming home late at night. I call Tony from my cell phone, and he looks out the back door, makes sure I get from the car to the house without any problem. Poor Julie."

I found myself annoyed by the general attitude that Julie could have done something—anything—to prevent being murdered. "Life is an uncertain business," I wrote. "I'm devastated by what has happened to Julie. But thinking that it wouldn't have happened if she'd had different friends, or if she'd had a burglar alarm, or if she hadn't crossed paths with a maniac— well, that's all just speculation. We'll have to wait and see what the police find out. We don't have enough facts to know why Julie was killed."

Despite the prevalence of murder in books and television, it's pretty unusual in real life. Most people are never touched by violent death, so the Food Group was upset. Each of us was hitting REPLY ALL two or three times a day.

The final round of e-mails set up plans for the group to attend Julie's funeral. It was to be "private," according to the *Grand Rapids Press*, but Jason called the funeral home and checked. We'd be welcome, he reported. It was to be at the home of Julie's grandmother in Grand Rapids. That caused a flurry of comment, but Jason told us the fabled Rachel Schrader was in poor health. "I guess it's hard for her to get out, especially in the winter," he wrote.

Lindy and I offered to pick up Margaret Van Meter as we drove through Holland, and the Denhams asked Carolyn Rose to go up with them. Jason said he had some errands to do before the service, so he went on his own.

As Lindy and I left for the funeral, the weather was as glum as our mood. January isn't the best month western Michigan has to offer, unless you're a cross-country skier, and that day seemed particularly dismal. It wasn't snowing, but the clouds looked cold enough to let loose a couple of inches any minute, and the temperature was around twenty degrees. Aunt Nettie had insisted we take her light blue Buick; I suppose it did look more suitable for a funeral than Lindy's bright green compact or my red minivan, the vehicle my dad had found to replace one that had been—well, shot to pieces—the previous fall.

In Holland, we almost got lost finding Margaret's house—an old two-story frame that looked as if it would be extremely drafty. Margaret opened the door and waved when we pulled into the drive. A moment later she climbed awkwardly into the backseat of the car. She had pulled a red stocking cap over her mousy brown hair, and she wore a bright red ski jacket that wasn't quite the same color as the hat. Her long corduroy skirt was purple, the worst possible color to wear with the red jacket. Obviously the red jacket was her only winter coat.

Suddenly I felt overdressed in my good leather

boots and the belted camel hair coat Aunt Nettie had given me for Christmas. Lindy, in a long navy blue flannel coat, looked neat and professional. Margaret looked like a hard-up mother of six small children. Then Margaret smiled her wonderful smile, and I thought how lucky those six kids were to have her home with them.

"Thanks for picking me up," Margaret said. "Jim really needed the van today."

"Who's keeping the kids?"

"My mother-in-law. She's really good about helping me out. She's highly upset over this murder. She acts like it's unpatriotic or something."

I didn't understand. "Unpatriotic?"

"Because it happened in good old reliable Holland. We never have murders here, according to her. She still thinks this is a Dutch farming community."

"Times do change," Lindy said. "And Holland has certainly changed since my grandparents lived here."

"Sure it has. But Gramma still thinks it's strange to see an aisle of Hispanic food in Meijer's. She's buying the rumor that some dark, swarthy guy was seen walking down the alley behind Julie's apartment."

Lindy's laugh didn't sound amused. "Well, Tony Herrera was home all night," she said.

The chill in her voice made me turn the heater up another notch and try to change the subject. "I know how to get to Grand Rapids, but do either of you know how to get to the Schrader house once we're there?"

"I printed out the directions Jason sent," Margaret said. "I never heard of having a funeral in a home before."

"I expect the Schrader house has plenty of room for a private funeral," Lindy said. "Jason says he tended bar at some benefit in that house once. He says there's a reception room the size of a ballroom."

The Schrader house also had a porte cochere, we learned when we pulled into the drive. The house was a classic Prairie style, and I wondered if it was an early Frank Lloyd Wright. Valet parking had been arranged, and inside the entrance hall uniformed maids were taking coats.

Lindy muttered in my ear as our coats disappeared, "If they hire this much help for a small private funeral, I want to cater somebody's birthday party."

We waited in the hall until Jason, Ronnie and Diane Denham, and Carolyn Rose appeared. Then we were escorted through a pair of double doors and into the big reception room Jason had described. It was nearly time for the service to start, and we were seated near the back, on folding chairs draped with white slipcovers.

The room was a good place for a small funeral service. No standard funeral sprays or wreaths were visible. The small platform that could have held musicians on another occasion was packed with greenery, and enormous baskets of white roses stood on either side of it. About seventy-five people were present. A musician at a grand piano in one corner played unobtrusively, and the minister sitting in a thronelike chair on the platform was tall and handsome enough to complete the picture. We already knew that Julie was to be cremated; we were to be spared the ghastly march past the coffin.

Everything was in perfect taste. I couldn't help thinking that Julie couldn't have planned it better herself. Julie might have been young, but she had been a traditionalist. She expected hostesses to get out the good silver and candles.

I'd seen no sign of the Schrader family's entrance, so I was surprised when the minister rose and called on us to pray. Where were they? There was no alcove that could have hidden them. I wondered if they were sitting at the back. Irreligiously, I sneaked a peek over my shoulder, and I found myself looking directly into a remarkable face.

It was the face of an old woman, and it looked as if that woman had suffered. She had beautiful white hair, and her face was heavily lined. She looked like the personification of grief. But Julie's snapping black eyes looked out from under her brows and met mine.

I should have looked away, but I was mesmerized. *That's what Julie would have looked like in fifty years*, I thought.

It was obviously Julie's grandmother.

I forced my head to twist around and face the right direction—I have a few manners—but I don't remember another thing about that service, except that it was brief. Twenty minutes was all it took to say good-bye to Julie Singletree.

Mrs. Schrader and the other family members must have slipped out during the final prayer, because the back row was empty when the minister dismissed us and I was able to look around again. As we left the room, a handsome and distinguished man I thought must be the funeral director greeted the mourners. He invited us across the hall, into a dining room where coffee, cookies, and finger sandwiches were offered. No elaborate wake was planned, I gathered.

The Food Group didn't know any of the other guests, of course, so we stood around talking to each other in subdued voices. In a few minutes we were approached by a young guy—he had dark hair and eyes like Julie's, but he was of normal height, not tiny as she had been. He wasn't bad looking, but his dark suit looked as if he'd slept in it, and he had a hangdog expression.

"We're glad you came," he said. His voice was high and almost squeaked. "I'm Julie's cousin, Brad Schrader."

Jason, who seemed to be taking leadership for the

occasion, introduced each of us. "We were in an informal networking group with Julie," he said. "All of us are in the food and party business."

Brad Schrader nodded. "Seventh Major Food Group? Julie told me about you guys."

"None of us knew her too well," Jason said.

"Julie and I were the only two kids in our generation, the last of the Schrader clan," Brad said. "We tried to keep in touch. But Julie was closer to your group than she was to me. She enjoyed your e-mails."

"Julie was the one who kept the group alive," Jason said. He didn't explain that Julie had more time to fool with e-mail than the rest of us did. Her business was just getting started; the rest of us were busy.

"Julie loved Warner Pier," Brad said. "Just the way I do. We both spent summers at Grandma's place down there when we were growing up. It's our real hometown."

"You grew up in Holland, too?" Carolyn Rose asked the question.

"Not me. Can't you tell by my accent? My dad was the Schrader kid who didn't go into the family firm. He moved to New York and worked in publishing, which made us the poor relations. I grew up in the Bronx. Julie's dad commuted to Grand Rapids and worked at Schrader Labs' main installation." He turned to me abruptly. "Miss McKinney? You're with TenHuis Chocolade?"

"Yes." I was surprised at being singled out.

"My grandmother wanted to meet you."

Brad Schrader made an awkward motion, pointing me toward the door into the next room, without so much as an "excuse me." He had apparently made his token gesture of hospitality to the group. He certainly lacked Julie's social skills. I felt rather sorry for him.

Brad pushed me through the next room—a living

room where about thirty mourners were standing around—then into a smaller sitting room. And all the way across the living room and into the smaller room I wondered why on earth Mrs. Schrader had singled me out. Was she a chocoholic hoping I had a few truffles in my pocket? Had she noticed me because I towered over all the other mourners? Was I going to be scolded for turning around during the opening prayer?

The small room was decorated in classic Craftsman style. Mrs. Schrader sat in a wheelchair beside a fire, which burned in a fireplace embellished with beautiful ceramic tiles I was willing to bet were original to the house. She gave me her hand graciously and signaled that I was to sit in a small chair pulled up beside her. Brad faded into the crowd.

When she spoke, her remark surprised me. "Are you Henry TenHuis's granddaughter?"

"Yes, I am." The light dawned. Mrs. Schrader owned property at Warner Pier, where my grandfather had operated a gas station. She must have been a customer. "He had the Lakeshore Service Station and Garage for thirty years."

"Yes, and I bought a lot of gasoline from him. But I knew him before that. We went to high school together."

"Oh! Yes, he did go to high school in Grand Rapids."

"He was two years ahead of me. I'll never forget how handsome he was in his Marine uniform. That would have been about 1944."

"I knew he served in the Pacific."

"I'm glad you know about him. He died young. Before you were born, I'm sure. But you have a certain look that reminds me of him."

I touched my hair. "I guess he passed on the blond gene. In all his pictures he looks very fair. I'm sorry I never knew him."

Just then the distinguished-looking man from the hall, the one I'd mentally pigeonholed as the funeral director, loomed over her. "Mother, the Johnsons are waiting to talk to you."

I managed not to gasp. This was no funeral director. He must be Martin Schrader, the uncle who discovered Julie's body.

"Mr. Johnson can't stay," he said. "You know his health . . ."

"I know." Mrs. Schrader sounded angry. "All my old friends are either dead or dying. Martin, this is Miss McKinney. You should remember her grandfather, Henry TenHuis."

Martin blinked. He was obviously trying to think who the hell Henry TenHuis was, and his mother was letting him squirm.

I took pity on him. "My grandfather had a garage and service station in Warner Pier back when gasoline cost considerably less than it does now. And I just learned that he went to high school with Mrs. Schrader."

Martin Schrader made a quick recovery. "Of course! I used to fill my bicycle tires at his station. Do you live in Warner Pier?"

His mother didn't give me time to answer the question. "I've been in the TenHuis Chocolade shop many times," she said. "Back before arthritis and heart trouble took all the pleasure out of my life. Philip TenHuis must be your uncle."

"Yes. But Uncle Phil is gone now, too. My aunt runs the shop."

Mrs. Schrader threw her head back defiantly. "And you have enough family feeling to go into the business. I suppose you are your aunt's heir."

I couldn't believe she'd asked such a rude question. I'm sure there was a long silence while I decided how to answer it. "The question doesn't arise," I said. "Aunt Nettie is the corpse—I mean, the core!

She's the core of the business! Without her skill as a chocolatier we have no product to sell."

I stood up. "It was extremely kind of you to talk with me, Mrs. Schrader. Julie loved and admired you greatly."

Her face crumpled. She took my hand, but this time it wasn't a gracious handclasp. It was a clutch. She grabbed the hand as if it were a lifeline. She tugged at it, and I found myself kneeling beside her chair while she whispered in my ear.

"I loved Julie," she said. "I loved her! She was darling! Why? Why? Why can't we keep the ones we love? Who can have wanted to take Julie away from me?"

I didn't have any answers, of course. All I could do was hold her hand in both of mine. "I don't know," I said. "I don't understand how this can have happened. We're all going to miss Julie terribly. I'm so sorry."

She nodded and turned away, producing a handkerchief from somewhere. I was dismissed. I rose as gracefully as I could, trying to remember how to get up from the Texas curtsy I had learned for beauty pageant competition. I moved away and an elderly couple took my place.

I started back into the big reception room, but someone touched my arm. It was Martin Schrader. I took a good look at him. He had a very high forehead, but once his hair began it was thick and silvery gray. He was—well, a handsome man. And he looked reliable. He'd be a perfect mouthpiece for a major company like Schrader Laboratories.

He spoke gravely. "Ms. TenHuis, I'd like to ask a favor. If I came down to Warner Pier, could we have dinner or lunch?"

I must have looked startled, because he went on hastily. "I need to talk to some of Julie's friends. Someone her own age."

"Actually, Mr. Schrader, I only met Julie a few times. Our friendship was mainly by e-mail."

"That's what I'm interested in." He leaned close. "The police think someone broke in to rob Julie. But I don't understand why the main thing he took was her computer."

Chapter 4

I guess I stared at him a minute. A computer didn't seem to me to be that odd a thing to steal, but this wasn't the place to discuss it. I moved back to his original question.

"I'll be happy to talk to you about Julie anytime, Mr. Schrader. It isn't necessary to take me out to lunch."

"Oh, but I'd like to." Was his smile wolfish? I decided it wasn't; it looked pleasant, just slightly harassed.

I smiled back insincerely. "I promised my finesse— I mean, my fiancé! I promised my fiancé that I'd cook dinner for him tonight. But any other time would be fine. Let me give you a card."

The mention of a fiancé didn't seem to disturb Martin Schrader. I gave him a TenHuis Chocolade card. By then some other guest was hovering, wanting his attention. I turned away and rejoined the Food Group. They all looked curious, so I explained that Mrs. Schrader had known my grandfather.

I didn't mention her son's invitation. In fact, as I thought his remarks over, I became determined to

make sure any meeting with Martin Schrader occurred in my office. Not that he had indicated any
interest in a social relationship. He'd given the impression of an uncle who was worried about his
niece's death. But why had he singled me out to talk
to? I didn't know Julie any better than any of the
other members of the Food Group did. In fact, I
thought Margaret had known her better than the rest
of us. They had lived in the same town, and Julie
had apparently dropped in on her often.

But Martin Schrader's request probably didn't
mean anything. He was upset over Julie's murder
and casting around for any scrap of information. At
least, I had convinced myself of that by the time we
had collected our coats and were standing under the
porte cochere waiting for the cars to be brought
around.

"Ms. McKinney?" The voice came from behind me.
It was barely audible, but I heard its distinctive
squeak. I turned to find Brad Schrader standing
there.

"I'm sorry to bother you," he said. "I wanted to
apologize for my uncle."

"Apologize?" Had Martin Schrader decided he
didn't want to talk to me after all and sent Brad with
his excuses?

Brad went on. "I saw him taking you aside. I hope
he wasn't . . . objectionable."

"He was very polite, Brad. Why did you think he'd
been objectionable?"

Brad looked down and shuffled his feet. "Well,
sometimes he . . ." Then he looked up, took a deep
breath, and spoke in a rush. "He's the family lech,
see. More or less a dirty old man. I wouldn't want
him to annoy you."

I had an impulse to laugh, but I managed to con-
tain it. "Don't worry, Brad. I can handle middle-aged

leches." I shook hands with him and told him again how sorry I was about Julie.

"I'll miss her e-mails," I said. "She was always sending something interesting."

Brad nodded. "She was on several lists," he said. "I guess that's where she got all that joke stuff."

"I didn't always have time to read the things she sent," I said. "But we probably all have a big file of her past messages. I can always go back and read them again."

That idea seemed to make Brad more morose than ever; he didn't reply, and I was out of small talk, too. Luckily, Aunt Nettie's blue Buick showed up then, and Lindy, Margaret, and I got into the car.

I waited until we were out of the driveway before I began to giggle. The thought of inept Brad trying to warn me off his poised and worldly uncle was simply laughable.

Of course, I had to explain my amusement to Lindy and Margaret.

"Huh," Lindy said. "Julie's relatives might be rich, but they're just as odd as mine."

"Mine are odd, too," Margaret said. "I asked my mom once if our family was crazier than anybody else's, and she said no. She said we just knew them better."

"Same here," I said. "If we're picking the oddest, I'd put my mom up against Uncle Martin and Cousin Brad combined. But one thing Martin Schrader said was really interesting. That part about talking to some of Julie's friends, to 'someone her own age.' "

"Why do you say that?" Lindy said.

"Think about that gathering we just left. Was there anybody there Julie's age?"

We all were silent for a few seconds. I was reviewing the crowd, and I guess Lindy and Margaret were, too, because they spoke at the same time.

"Not really," Lindy said.

"Just a few," Margaret said. "There was that group that clustered around the couches in the big room. They looked younger than most. But I eavesdropped on them, and I think they all worked for Schrader Labs. One of them was Martin Schrader's secretary."

"Maybe Julie's friends are having a separate service—more of a wake or a party," Lindy said. "That's what Warner Pier's artsy crowd does sometimes."

"Maybe so," I said. "If Julie went to high school in Holland, you'd think some of her friends would still be around."

"There aren't too many of us," Margaret said.

I swiveled my head toward her. "Did you go to high school with Julie?"

"Yes. Didn't either of us ever mention it?"

"No. I thought you met through some party or wedding."

"Julie and I graduated from Holland Christian the same year. But we didn't run in the same crowd. I really got to be friends with her during the past year."

"Maybe her friends are not high-toned enough for the Schraders," Lindy said. "Maybe they deliberately didn't invite them to the funeral."

We all thought it over again, but it was Margaret who finally said what we were all thinking—right out loud. "Julie was so cute. You'd think she would have had a boyfriend."

But none of us could think of any boyfriend-type person at the service.

"You know," I said, "thinking back to the Food Group e-mails, Julie never mentioned a boyfriend, did she? In fact, we never learned much about her personal life."

"You're right," Lindy said. "She never had much to say about herself. When Diane and Ronnie became grandparents again, they put a message out right away. When Tony Junior made the honor roll for the first time, I told everybody I saw, and I put a message on the Food Group list. Even you, Lee. You've mentioned working on the new apartment several times."

"And I let everybody know when I was so worried because Jim's hours got cut back," Margaret said. "And Jason—he told about the horrible weekend he spent painting his living room, when it rained and the paint wouldn't dry. But Julie—she never said a word about herself. Just weddings and parties she was planning and all that philosophical stuff."

"Strange," I said.

"Odd," Lindy said.

"Weird," Margaret said. "But I can understand Julie not wanting to talk about her relatives. If the uncle is a lech, the cousin is a nerd, and the grandmother is bossy as all get out . . . well, if you can't say anything good, shut up."

We shut up. Or at least we changed the subject. Lindy and Margaret traded stories about their kids, and I kept my mouth shut and concentrated on the road. That was because it began to snow just as we reached the southern edge of Grand Rapids.

Since I was raised in Texas, I didn't get a lot of experience driving in snow when I was growing up. Now ice, yes, Texas usually has a couple of dandy ice storms every winter. I've seen some horrible sleet and freezing rain around both my hometowns, Dallas and Prairie Creek. But thick, heavy snow is strange to me. It makes me nervous.

I reminded myself that Michigan highways are well maintained—we saw several snowplows during the trip—that Aunt Nettie's Buick was a good, heavy car with the proper tires for driving in snow, and that I was smart enough not to hit the brakes suddenly or spin my tires trying to start up. But I was still nervous, maybe because I was afraid I'd do something stupid rather than because I was afraid I'd have a wreck. Though having a wreck in somebody else's car is not high on the list of the things I want to do.

But we didn't have a wreck. The only bad moments were three or four times when semis passed us going a million miles an hour and threw sheets of snow onto our windshield. The road didn't get too bad, though it snowed harder—naturally—the further south and west we went. It's called "lake effect snow." Tradition has it that the closer you get to Lake Michigan, the heavier the snowfall gets, and it's true. I've read a scientific explanation for this, but don't ask me to repeat it.

We dropped Margaret off in Holland, then drove on to Warner Pier. I took Lindy to the big old house she and Tony had moved into right before Christmas. Tony Junior and his chocolate lab, Monte, came out on the porch to greet us. Lindy invited me in, but I declined, and she put her hand on the door handle.

"Gosh!" she said. "I'll always wonder if the killer was in Julie's apartment when I went by there that night."

"What! You were at Julie's apartment the night she was killed? Have you told the police?"

"I told Chief Jones. He said he'd pass it along to the Holland detectives, and they might want to talk to me. He said I shouldn't mention it, so don't tell anybody else."

"What were you doing there?"

"I went up to visit Maria Nunez at Holland Hospital. You know, the gray-haired waitress at the Sidewalk Café. She had pneumonia, but she's better now. Anyway, I was coming back by Food Fare, and I realized I was near Julie's. So I stopped."

"When was this?"

"About nine o'clock. It was kind of late to drop in

on somebody, so I just knocked once. She didn't come to the door, and I went away."

"So you didn't see anything suspicious?"

"It was dead silent, Lee. Oh! That's not a good choice of words, is it? But I couldn't see into the apartment at all. It's not as if the window blinds were open or anything. All I saw was the parking lot."

"And there was no car in it that bristled with axes and guns, huh?"

"Nope. I slipped and fell into a really weird, bug-eyed car that was parked backward, but it probably belonged to one of the other tenants. And you know me, it could have been a Rolls-Royce, and I wouldn't have known the difference."

I laughed. Lindy's indifference to cars is legendary among her friends. Her husband swears he puts an Indiana University pennant on her antenna, even though she's not a Hoosier fan, because Lindy would never find her car in a parking lot if it didn't have a red-and-white flag on it.

I promised Lindy I wouldn't say anything about her visit to Julie's apartment; then I left, saying I wanted to check on TenHuis Chocolade before it closed up.

Which was a fib. Actually, I wanted to call Joe Woodyard. I was supposed to see him shortly, but I wanted to talk to him right that minute. I wanted to tell him about the strange funeral for a nice girl who apparently had several peculiar relatives, but no friends. I wanted to tell him Uncle Martin wanted me to go out to dinner with him, and I felt uneasy about going, but I couldn't say exactly why, and, no, it wasn't because nerdy Cousin Brad told me Martin was a lech. The whole day had been strange, and I wanted to talk about it with someone who cared.

So I drove carefully to TenHuis Chocolade, parked in front of the shop and went in. I waved to Aunt

Nettie, inhaled six deep breaths of chocolate aroma, helped myself to a Dutch caramel bonbon ("Soft, creamy, European-style caramel in dark chocolate"), then went to the telephone.

Naturally, I couldn't find Joe. He wasn't at his boat shop. He wasn't at his apartment. He didn't answer his cell phone.

We had a date for seven o'clock, when he was supposed to come out to the house I shared with Aunt Nettie. I really had promised I'd cook dinner for him. But we'd made that plan after Hogan Jones had asked Aunt Nettie to go out to dinner with him that evening. Would the snow change their plans? Would it change ours? Aunt Nettie and I saw enough of each other without double dating.

I was still wondering when Aunt Nettie came into the office. She looked serious. "How were the roads?"

"Not too bad."

"It's supposed to stop pretty soon. Hogan and I still plan on going into Holland for dinner."

That was one of my questions answered. But before I could react, Aunt Nettie pulled a bright pink envelope out of the pocket of her white, heavy duty food service apron. "I got an unexpected letter," she said. "I wanted to show it to you."

"Who's it from?"

"My sister-in-law. My brother's widow. Read it."

She shoved the envelope across the desk. It was not only bright pink, but the flap was scalloped and printed to look like lace. I opened it. The notepaper was scalloped to match, and it also had tiny hearts dancing across the top.

" 'Dear Nettie,' " I read. " 'I know we haven't been in touch much since Ed died, but you've always been good about remembering Bobby at Christmas and on his birthday. Plus when he graduated from high school. I have appreciated it.

" 'Well, Bobby is now close to graduating from Eastern Michigan. He's majored in marketing, and he's done pretty good. He has worked part-time as a waiter, and I'm proud of him. Since he's my only chick, I guess I ought to be!

" 'Anyway, you said in your Christmas letter that the business is back on track and you and Phil's niece were thinking of expanding. Will you need to hire someone around June? It would be such a good opportunity for Bobby!

" 'I'm sorry to be so pushy, but I'd never forgive myself if Bobby missed such a good chance to be involved in a successful family business.

" 'I'm doing fine. The plant has had some layoffs, but so far my job seems safe.

" 'Love, Corrine.' "

So help me, as I read those final words, I could hear Mrs. Schrader's voice echoing in my ear. "I suppose you are your aunt's heir."

It took me a minute to form a reply. And then I blew it.

"It would have made a better imposition if Bobby had sent a recipe himself," I said.

Usually Aunt Nettie can figure out what I was trying to say, but that one confused her completely. She looked at me with an expression of openmouthed incomprehension.

In fact, my statement had thrown me completely. For a moment I didn't have the slightest idea myself what I'd been trying to say. Then I began to scramble. "I mean—I mean—Bobby would have made a better impression if he had written and sent his résumé himself."

Aunt Nettie's face smoothed into its usual placid contours. "I agree," she said. "I haven't seen Bobby in years. I have no idea whether or not he'd be a good worker."

"I wonder if Bobby knows his mom wrote you. He

might not even be interested in a clerical job. And that's what we need. Or what I need. I could use somebody to help with the orders and shipments and to handle the front counter. Or did you have something else in mind?"

"I didn't really have anything specific in mind, Lee. Corinne has always acted like I was completely helpless without Phil. When I wrote her at Christmas—well, I guess I was trying to brag a little. After all, we were finally able to begin paying ourselves full salaries! I must have overdone it."

"We're entitled to brag a little," I said. "Last year was the best TenHuis Chocolade ever had."

"What do you think we should do?"

"*You* should do? About Bobby? Talk to him, I guess. The problem with family members is that they're easy to hire, but hard to fire. I marvel that you had the nerve to hire me."

"That was an easy decision. You'd worked here earlier. I knew you were a hard worker and had a head for figures."

"And I needed a job."

"Well, if you'd been chief accountant for IBM, I wouldn't have had the courage to offer you this little job." She looked at me seriously. "Lee, I know you are capable of much more important things than shipping TenHuis chocolates around the country. When that big opportunity comes, I want you to take it."

"Are you trying to get rid of me?"

"No! No! But I know things can't go on forever. Your life will change. My life will, too."

After that unsettling remark, she left the office.

Getting married was all the change I could contemplate right at that moment. But Aunt Nettie had confused me. Somehow, I felt that conversation wasn't only about her nephew Bobby and the possibility that he might want a job.

I picked up the phone and punched the speed dial for Joe's boat shop again. Now I desperately wanted to talk to him. More than my day was messed up; my whole life seemed to be.

But Joe was still not at home, not at work, not answering his cell phone. I angrily went through the mail and the phone messages. I was concentrating so hard on my disappointment over not reaching him that I jumped about a foot when the phone rang.

"Hi," Joe said.

"Where are you?"

"City hall."

"City hall? You never go to city hall on Mondays."

"I had a little emergency and needed to use the city phone. When did you get back?"

"About an hour ago. Are we still having dinner?"

"I was counting on it."

"Good. I need to talk to somebody."

"Now?"

I checked the time. Five o'clock. "I guess I can wait until I see you. I just need a sympathetic ear."

"So do I. This afternoon has been nutso."

"What's wrong?"

"Just a little e-mail problem."

"E-mail!"

"I'll tell you about it when I see you. If six isn't too early?"

I said six was fine, and Joe hung up.

E-mail? Joe was having a problem with e-mail?

I thought e-mail was supposed to enhance communications. But it had indirectly linked me with some very unusual people. And now it was a problem for Joe.

Huh.

CHOCOLATE CHAT

LITERARY CHOCOLATE

"Venice is like eating an entire box of chocolate liqueurs in one go."   —Truman Capote

"My momma always said life was like a box of chocolates. You never know what you're gonna get."
—Forrest Gump

"What use are cartridges in battle? I always carry chocolate instead."   —George Bernard Shaw

"Chocolate is a perfect food, as wholesome as it is delicious, a beneficent restorer of exhausted power. It is the best friend of those engaged in literary pursuits."
—Baron Justus von Liebig

Chapter 5

Aunt Nettie was still dressing when I heard Chief Hogan Jones pull into the drive. I guess she heard the car, too, because she stuck her head out her bedroom door. "Lee! Can you talk to Hogan a minute?"

"Sure. Keep on primping."

Aunt Nettie giggled. Since she had started dating after three years of widowhood, she really had become like a girl again. And she was dating Hogan Jones—the catch of the Warner Pier older crowd.

Aunt Nettie hires a man with a snowplow to keep her drive cleared. Since everybody uses our back porch as an entry, especially during the winter, the man also keeps the short flagstone walk cleared. Luckily, he'd come that afternoon. I met Hogan at the kitchen door. It had occurred to me that he might know something I wanted to know, and I was pleased to have the opportunity to ask him.

When I opened the door Hogan was stamping his boots on the sidewalk.

"Come on in," I said. "Aunt Nettie's almost ready, but you and I get to talk for a minute."

"I need some calm conversation to settle my nerves after the drive out here. That new drop-off on Lake Shore Drive is a doozy."

Lake Shore Drive, of course, gets its name because it runs right along the shore of Lake Michigan. This is nice, in general, but if we have a winter with lots of west wind, there's a drawback. Big chunks of ice—six or eight feet thick—form along the shore. They break off and float out into the water. Then a west wind comes and drives them right back to the lake's edge, where they grind away at the beach and bank like bulldozers. That winter the ice had eaten the bank away at one spot until it was right up to the pavement. Get an inch too close to the edge, and the car would go tumbling down. The street department had put up a barricade, of course, but it didn't look very substantial.

"You're chief of police," I said. "Call the street department and tell 'em it's a safety hazard."

"I already told them, and they already knew. But they're trying to get some more concrete barriers. Until they can get hold of some, they're stuck with that orange tape and a few wooden barriers with big spaces between."

"Well, since you made it safely, I wanted to ask you a question."

"I hope it's not about Julie Singletree." Hogan stepped inside the kitchen and wiped his boots on the throw rug. Hogan is in his midsixties, and he's not handsome, but he has an appeal I can appreciate. It's something about his close resemblance to Abraham Lincoln in both height and rugged features. He looks reliable, intelligent, humorous, and macho.

"Why don't you want me to ask about Julie's death?" I said. "After all, Julie was a friend, or at least an acquaintance, of mine."

I gestured toward the living room, and Hogan followed me, frowning. "I don't have any excuse for getting interested in a crime that happened in another city," he said.

"I did appreciate your getting some details for me the day after she was killed. But I'm not asking you to do that again. This time I just wanted an opinion."

"I got lots of those. And they're worth every cent you pay for 'em."

"I went to Julie's funeral today—the whole Food Group did—and Julie's uncle told me her computer was stolen from her apartment."

"So?"

"So, he said he found this very strange. But why? Isn't a computer a common thing to steal? Like TV sets or CD players? Anything easy to hock?"

Hogan frowned. "I don't know that there's a general rule about burglars, but yeah, they've been known to take computers."

"Then why was Martin Schrader surprised?"

"Maybe he's just dumb about how burglars operate." The chief's eyes shifted as he spoke, and I looked at him closely.

"Do you know what else was taken?"

"Not everything. Like I said, I don't really have any excuse to ask about it."

"Aw, c'mon, Hogan. Don't try to tell me cops don't gossip just like the rest of us."

He grinned. "You know better than that, Lee." Then he sighed. "I guess it won't hurt to tell you what I heard on the grapevine. The word is that the burglar or killer or whoever it was didn't take much. Just a few things. And he messed the apartment up some."

"Like he'd been searching for something?"

"No, like he didn't care if he left a mess behind him. Some drawers were pulled out. A couple of things were turned over." Hogan cleared his throat. "The Holland detectives think he probably came on foot."

"Did they find tracks?"

"Sure. Thousands. Julie lived in an apartment complex, remember? Nobody left the track of a size fifteen extra wide Nike on her carpet, if that's what you mean."

"In other words, the tracks aren't any help. I suppose there aren't any fingerprints either."

"Fingerprints are never any help unless you find somebody to match them with. And then you have to prove that somebody was never in the apartment at any other time, for any other reason."

By now Hogan and I were sitting in chairs in front of the brick fireplace in the living room. He pointed to the wood stacked inside. "Do you want me to start you a fire?"

"No, thanks. Joe's coming over. He likes to do it. All you guys are fire builders."

Hogan smiled. "I hope he can cheer you up, Lee. I know that having a friend killed is a real jolt. All I can tell you is that it does look as if somebody broke in, probably some kind of burglar. My guess is that Julie surprised him, he panicked and hit her."

"She was a little thing, Hogan. A foot shorter than I am. It wouldn't have been hard to kill her."

He nodded. "Yeah. My Holland buddy told me that. Anyway, the burglar must have decided to get out of there in a hurry."

"Where did the tale about the dark guy walking down the alley come from?" Hogan looked surprised, and I repeated the gossip Lindy and I had gotten from Margaret Van Meter.

Hogan shrugged. "I hadn't heard that one. But I doubt a witness would have seen if a guy walking down the alley was dark or fair or in between. The temperature was close to zero that night. If the guy wasn't wearing a heavy jacket and hat, his hair and skin would have been the color of ice. Anyway, the Holland detectives think the killer just took the few things he could carry in one trip, which makes them think he was on foot."

"He wouldn't have wanted to look like Santa with his pack."

"Right. He couldn't have carried anything too bulky. Which might be why he took the computer, but not the monitor or the keyboard—"

"Monitor or keyboard? But Julie had a laptop! She had it along the day she came down to see the mouse samples she ordered for the Schrader banquet."

"There were two computers. She had that flashy new Gateway she carried around to plan parties with. It's still there. And she had an old Macintosh that she used for correspondence and e-mail."

"That's a weird way to manage your computer life."

"Maybe not. She kept the Macintosh connected to the phone line. The laptop was in a brief case."

"And it wasn't stolen?"

"The laptop was inside the case and stashed in a closet. The burglar probably didn't realize what it was."

"You say the killer didn't take the Macintosh keyboard? What else did he take?"

"I didn't hear the whole list. Her jewelry box was gone. The descriptions are circulating. Her grandmother and uncle say she just had a few family pieces."

"Their idea of a 'few family pieces' might include the Kohinoor. So nothing else is missing?"

Hogan laughed. "No, there's more. But I haven't seen a list. All I know about specifically is her mouse."

"You mean the killer took her computer and mouse, but not the keyboard?"

"Not a computer mouse. A real mouse."

"Julie had a mouse?"

"Apparently it's a Schrader family tradition. My

buddy was laughing about it. The Schrader lab originally did a lot of testing involving mice, and the family members all think they're wonderful pets. So Julie had a pet mouse, a white one. She kept it in a fish tank in the living room. The tank got knocked over, and the mouse escaped. It hasn't been found."

"Oh, my gosh! That'll come as a surprise to the next tenants."

"Her uncle set a trap—you know, one of these live traps—and left it there. I assure you that the Holland PD doesn't want the mouse as evidence. As soon as it turns up, they'll call the uncle."

"One of the Holland cops will probably open a drawer, and it'll pop out and scare him to death."

Hogan and I chuckled over the fate of the Holland detectives who had to search Julie's apartment, knowing that a mouse might scurry out at any moment. Even a small, tame, white mouse could be pretty surprising if you looked under the couch and found it looking back at you.

We were still chuckling when Aunt Nettie came out. Hogan complimented her appearance—she did look rosy and pretty—and they left. I put a card table up in the living room and set it for dinner in front of the fireplace. I was sure Joe would want to have a fire, and we might as well enjoy it.

I couldn't help thinking about Julie. Poor little Julie, so small and easy to kill. A tear welled up, and I had to get a tissue. I moved to the sink, scrubbed the baking potatoes seriously, then stabbed them vigorously with a paring knife. Pretending I was giving Julie's killer a few whacks made me feel a little better. The tears had stopped by the time I had the potatoes and meatloaf in the 400-degree oven.

Meatloaf and baked potatoes—not exciting, but one of Joe's favorite meals. He tells me anybody can tell he and I were both raised in moderate circumstances. We both like meatloaf, hot dogs and sauerkraut, porcupine meatballs, and even tuna casserole. As a Texan, I've introduced him to taco salad and chicken-fried steak with cream gravy, and he seems to like those, too. He'd better.

The house smelled pretty good by the time Joe slammed the door of his pickup and came up the back walk, stamping his feet the way Hogan had. He was clutching what was obviously a bottle in a paper sack in his left hand. We greeted each other affectionately, though Joe used only one arm.

"You didn't have a great day, I guess," Joe said after I'd been kissed thoroughly.

"Not until now. But it doesn't sound as if you did either. How come you had to spend time at city hall? You usually limit your city attorney business to Tuesdays."

"Actually, I usually work on it some every day, but I work at home. A little reading and some e-mail. But today a minor flap blew up, and I had to do some telephoning. It involved a conference call, and that's easier to do with the city hall phones."

"What happened?"

Joe plucked a bottle of Michigan red out of his paper sack. "How about a glass of wine before I tell you?"

"Sure. I set the table up in the living room, in case you want to have a fire."

"You open the wine; I'll light the fire."

Joe's work life might be described as bipolar. He finished Warner Pier High as "most likely to succeed"—class president, plus state honors in debate and wrestling. He kept up his scholastic and leadership record at the University of Michigan, and sailed into law school. His mother—who owns a Warner Pier insurance agency—thought he was headed for a career in corporate law. But after he graduated, Joe amazed and annoyed her by going to work for a legal aid nonprofit. Then he married a woman who was one of the nation's most famous—or maybe infamous—defense attorneys, a confidante to the rich and famous. Joe doesn't talk about her unless I ask, but she must have nearly wrecked his life. At least she wrecked his love for the practice of law. After two years of marriage he quit law, got a divorce, and opened a boat shop, specializing in the restoration of antique wooden speedboats.

"Honest craftsmanship," he had told me. "The best way to keep your self-respect."

But a few months earlier he'd edged back into law when he took a part-time job as city attorney for Warner Pier. He supposedly gave them the equivalent of one day of work a week. He had taken the job because of me, and I wasn't sure I liked that. He had been making so little money in the boat business that he hadn't felt he could ask me to marry him. The part-time job paid for an apartment in downtown Warner Pier, an apartment we'd be sharing in three more months.

But I didn't want Joe to feel that he had to compromise on how he wanted to run his life because of me. The idealism that had driven him out of the practice of law was one of the things I liked about him. My father was an auto mechanic; I would be perfectly content with a craftsman as a husband. Besides, I'd tried the upscale life during my first marriage, and I didn't like it.

But I tried to put all this aside when I carried a tray with crackers and cheese and two glasses of wine into the living room. The couch has a good view of the fire, and we settled down on it.

"What's this e-mail problem you had?" I said.

Joe laughed. "It's not really an 'e-mail' problem. It's an 'e-go' problem."

"Ego? Yours?"

"Not this time. Have I told you about Ellison Peters?"

THE CHOCOLATE MOUSE TRAP 49

"Is he on that e-mail list of small town city attorneys?"

"Oh, yeah. But he's a cut above the rest of us. The 'small town' he represents is St. Anthony. You know, 'Tony City.' "

"Over by Detroit?"

"It's the place people move to when they want to go upscale from Grosse Pointe. We may think we have lots of millionaires around here, but Tony City makes Warner Pier look like the low-rent district."

"And Ellison thinks his city's economic status gives him clout?"

"Definitely. Not that he has the money to live there himself. But he's one of these with a slick suit, a slick haircut, and a slick car."

"But is he a slick lawyer?"

"He's a pretty good lawyer. Just a shade too dignified for me to invite him out to the boat shop. Anyway, he has appointed himself chairman of the small town city attorneys e-mail list."

"What did he do to cause a problem?"

"He's decided we should present a case at a moot court competition. He committed us without consulting the rest of the list." Joe laughed. "Some of the other guys aren't very excited about it."

"If he can't get enough people to take part, he can't pull it off. Why is this a problem?"

"There was a lot of e-mailing back and forth when it came up." Joe laughed again. "And some of the people failed to remove all the old messages before they sent new ones."

I began to see. "Oh, no!"

"Oh, yes. The word 'idiot' was used."

We both laughed. "Then you," I said, "had to spend the afternoon on the phone calming this guy down."

"Right. It took a conference call between four of

us. But we got Ellison to climb off his high horse. It's all going to work out."

Then Joe got up and poked at his fire. He was looking in the fireplace, not at me, when he spoke again. "All the guys on the list want invitations to the wedding."

There went the evening, right down the drain.

Chapter 6

D arn. Joe had obviously come with a new array of arguments designed to get me to agree to a big wedding.

"I'd better check on the meatloaf," I said. I got up and went to the kitchen.

I fled the living room because I didn't want to argue about it. Again. Oh, I knew we had to settle the issue sometime, but not that night. I got angry at the thought.

Besides, a tricky little voice told me, if I waited long enough we wouldn't have time to plan a big wedding before April, and Joe would have to give the idea up.

I had looked at the meatloaf and turned the fire on low under the green beans when I heard Joe coming.

Joe spoke slowly. "Did I say something wrong?"

"Oh, no. I'm just upset tonight. The funeral and everything."

"Are you sure?"

"Positive. I've put the fire under the green beans—Texas style, with bacon bits. We can have another glass of wine."

Joe looked concerned, but again I told myself I didn't want to discuss the wedding plans that night. I led the way to the living room and tried to change the subject.

"Julie's family is a bit strange," I said.

"How so?"

I described the funeral and the reception afterward, including my tête-à-tête with Rachel Schrader, and ending with Uncle Martin's declaration that he wanted to discuss Julie with "someone her own age."

"Actually," I said, "I'm not Julie's age. I'm at least five years older. Or at least I thought I was. Julie's age wasn't in her obituary. But I found out today she went to high school with Margaret. Margaret knows her a lot better than I do, actually."

Joe laughed. "Margaret's the one with six kids, right? She might not be nearly as interesting to Martin Schrader as a gorgeous six-foot beauty queen."

Suddenly I was as angry as ever, and all my intentions of not discussing how angry I had been flew away. "Gorgeous six-foot beauty queen! You sound just like my mother."

Joe looked taken aback. "Your mother? Why?"

"The only reason I got into the beauty pageant business was my mother. She pushed and pushed. She kept telling me it would help my self-esteem, give me confidence."

"You seem to have plenty of both. Maybe it worked."

"No! It destroyed both. How would you like having a pageant director tell you to work on your inner thighs? Having the musical director tell you not to worry about your tiny, weak little voice because he can beef it up with the sound system? I may have learned how to fake confidence, but if I have any self-esteem, it's because I learned to stand up for myself and tell the beauty business—and my mother—to go jump."

Joe sipped his wine, then put the glass down on the coffee table. Then he turned toward me, but leaned back in the corner of the couch. "Did I ever tell you that you have a beautiful—" he paused and cleared his throat—"mind?"

I looked at him narrowly. "Just don't forget that," I said.

Then we were both laughing, and I had laid my head on his shoulder, and he had put his arms around me.

"Am I wrong in thinking I brought this on by talking about our wedding plans?" Joe said.

"You made me think of my mom, I guess, and she's a major reason that I don't want a big wedding. Besides, Joe, I'm almost thirty years old. I'm too old to be a blushing bride."

He pulled me closer. "I don't expect you to blush for anybody but me. But that's beside the point. Your problem with the wedding isn't really about your parents."

"I thought it was."

"No, it's about something more important. It's about you spending fifteen years of your life avoiding confrontation with your parents."

"That's silly! My mother and I argue all the time."

"No, you don't. You get mad at your mother all the time, but you never tell her what you think. You haven't really told her to 'go jump.' You've just started avoiding sensitive topics."

"I don't think I do that."

"Remember Christmas? We wanted to spend Christmas Day with her, then go to Prairie Creek to see your dad the day after. But she said we'd have to do it the other way around so she could stay over a day in Hong Kong. All you said was, 'Yes, Mother.' "

"Why fight about it? She's entitled to her plans."

"Yes, but those plans forced us into spending

Christmas Day with your stepmother's family. We didn't have a chance to really talk to your dad until late that night, and only for a short time. And having us show up a day early annoyed Annie and her daughter."

"They're always annoyed with me over something."

"I don't think Annie was annoyed with you. She was mad at your mom."

"Why?"

"Because your mom forced us to change our plans and our new plans interfered with Annie's family reunion. Now, Brenda's another case. Brenda's just flat jealous of you."

"Jealous! Why?"

Joe hugged me tighter. "Because your dad loves you best."

I stared. "But he's my dad! He's just her stepdad."

"Does Brenda have a father?"

"Well, he's never around."

"I noticed she didn't get a Christmas present from him."

I sighed. "I guess it is pretty hard on her."

"Besides, you're the beauty queen. You're the one who graduated from college with really good grades. You're the one who can wrap your dad around your finger with the flicker of an eyelash."

"You make me sound awful!"

"From Brenda's viewpoint, you are. She can't possibly compete for your dad's attention when you're around. And all it takes is a phone call from you and he drops everything and buys you a car."

"I paid for it! He just found it for me."

"And drove it to St. Louis for you to pick up."

"Well, I notice he found a good car for Brenda's high school graduation present. And I bet she didn't have to pay for it."

"We've gotten way off the subject I thought we ought to talk about."

"Oh? I thought we were analyzing my relations with my family."

"Oh, it's a much broader subject than that. We're analyzing your relations with me and my relations with you."

"That's a more interesting subject, I guess."

"I hope so." Joe stopped talking and gave me a kiss. "But our interpersonal relations worry me sometimes."

"Why?"

"Because sometimes you treat me like you treat your mother."

"My mother!"

"Yes. You avoid confrontation. You let me have my way—sometimes—because you don't want to argue about it."

"If it's something I don't care about . . ."

"Then say, 'I don't care.' And say it as if you mean it. Don't refuse to discuss something because you're afraid we'll argue over it. And don't stonewall me just as a way to win an argument."

He'd seen right through me, right through to that tricky little voice that told me if I stalled long enough the wedding issue would decide itself. I didn't know what to say.

But I didn't have to say anything, because Joe gave me a kiss that I'll remember a long time. Then he patted my fanny gently. "Think about it, okay? But we don't have to talk about it anymore tonight. Nothing should interfere with meatloaf."

"First things first, huh?"

"I've got *my* priorities straight."

It's easy to see why I fell for this guy. A little later I got up and went to the kitchen to finish up the dinner. Joe followed me. He stood in the doorway and watched me slice the meatloaf and get the baked potatoes out of the oven.

"What did you tell Martin Schrader?" he said.

"When he wanted to talk to me about Julie? What could I say? I told him I would." Then I finished up the story, telling Joe about Brad Schrader's warning.

"Are you uneasy about meeting Martin Schrader?" Joe asked.

"Not really. I'm certainly not going to meet him at a lonely cabin in the woods, like the naive heroine of a romantic novel. But I wouldn't be afraid to talk to him in my office or in a restaurant. Of course, I might want to drive my own car to the restaurant."

"And you'll wear a business suit." Joe grinned.

"My black pants suit and the heavy boots with the chunky heels. The modern suit of armor. Ready for battle." I picked up the dinner plates, already served, and gestured at the salad with my elbow. Joe obediently lifted it and followed me into the living room.

"Joe," I said. "You've lived around Warner Pier most of your life, and Martin Schrader has been around here all of his—at least in the summers. Is he notorious as a skirt chaser?"

"I never heard of it. But I was gone nearly ten years. Besides, I definitely don't move in the same circles he does. I'll ask Mom. She sells the summer people a lot of insurance, and she doesn't do it by ignoring who lives next door to whom and who's seen having dinner with whom."

The rest of the evening was ordinary. Joe and I talked about the wedding, decided to send his mother flowers on her birthday, argued about what the city council should do to try to solve the Warner Pier parking problem, then touched on the old house Lindy and Tony had bought. We were doing the dishes when Aunt Nettie and Hogan came home. We lingered in the kitchen, so they could have the living room, and Joe went home before eleven.

I stay over with Joe sometimes, but he rarely stays with me. The house Aunt Nettie and I share simply doesn't have any privacy. The walls are so thin that a conversation anyplace upstairs is plainly audible downstairs. And there's not a lot of space. Aunt Nettie had talked about putting in a second bathroom, upstairs, but since I was planning to move out, she dropped the idea.

I'd just gotten into my pajamas when the phone rang. I answered the upstairs extension.

"Lee?" It was Joe. "When I drove by Mom's house she was still up, so I stopped and asked her about Martin Schrader. She told me something interesting."

"*Is* Martin a notorious skirt chaser?"

"Not really. She knew of only one person he'd dated locally. Carolyn Rose."

I nearly dropped the phone. Carolyn Rose? The florist member of the Seventh Major Food Group.

"Ye gods!" I said. "At the funeral this afternoon, he didn't speak to her at all. They acted like complete strangers."

"All Mom knew is that when Carolyn first opened her shop—that's more than five years ago—she came to Mom for insurance. And she told Mom she was moving to Warner Pier because it was close to her 'boyfriend.' Mom said she almost bragged about who he was—Martin Schrader."

"I guess he didn't turn out to be the marrying kind."

"Not if that's what she wanted . . ."

Joe and I said good night, and I climbed into my bed, stared at the ceiling, and thought about Carolyn Rose. It was more fun than thinking about the issues Joe had raised about my personality.

Carolyn had an interesting personality, too. Outwardly, she was a tough businesswoman. Maybe her name should be "Thorne," rather than "Rose." I wondered if she had really cared about Martin

Schrader, or if she was attracted by his financial attributes.

Martin would be considered quite a catch, of course, if you were looking for a successful man from a prominent family. And he was certainly attractive. But he had to be at least in his fifties and apparently he'd never married; he was definitely in the confirmed bachelor category. And the way his mother sat on him would give any girlfriend pause for thought.

One thing was for certain, I concluded before I picked up my bedtime book. I would never mention Martin Schrader to Carolyn Rose.

I was barely out of bed the next morning when the phone rang again. It was Joe. He'd forgotten he had to make a quick trip to Lansing on city business that day. Could I order the flowers for his mother's birthday?

"Tell Carolyn to send me the bill," he said.

"Sure," I said. And as I said it, I'll swear, the thing that popped into my mind was, "That'll be a good excuse to talk to Carolyn Rose about Martin Schrader." When I realized what I'd been thinking, I shuddered. I definitely did not want to talk to Carolyn Rose about Martin Schrader. Or that's what I told myself.

I went by House of Roses on my way to work. Of course, I could have taken care of the whole thing on the phone, but somehow—despite my resolution of the night before—I decided it would be friendlier if I went by personally. I took the precaution of rehearsing what I wanted to say beforehand. I didn't want my tangled tongue tripping me up, producing "Martin," as in Schrader, when I'd meant to say "marguerite," as in daisy.

House of Roses is located in a late-Victorian cottage on the state highway that skirts Warner Pier. Carolyn had battled the planning commission until she got permission to give it a trendy, "painted lady" look, with the siding a brilliant yellow and the trim orange, green, and pink. I knew that Carolyn kept very few flowers in stock during the winter months; she wasn't going to get much drop-in business in a town of just 2,500.

I was almost surprised to see an SUV that wasn't Carolyn's parked in her graveled—and snow-covered—parking area. Carolyn's only vehicle was the panel truck with "House of Roses" on the side. I parked beside the SUV and waded to the porch, where I stamped the snow off my boots.

Inside, the shop was chopped up into a lot of small rooms. It smelled like flowers, even though most of the arrangements in sight were artificial. There was a Valentine's Day display, of course, which featured some fresh red and white carnations and a few silk roses. The specialty foods area, with fancy nuts and crackers, looked tired. Winter is definitely an off time for retailers in a beach resort town.

I didn't see either Carolyn or the driver of the SUV when I came in. I called out, and Carolyn's head of fake red hair poked out of a back room. "Hi, Lee," she said. "Come to rehash the funeral?"

"Actually, I'm detailed to order flowers for Joe's mom's birthday."

"Good. You're my first customer. And my computer's on the fritz. Jack Ingersoll is here working on it." That explained the SUV. Jack ran a computer service from his home in Warner Pier, though most of his clients were from elsewhere.

Carolyn was coming out from the back. "Let me give you a cup of coffee while we talk about Mercy's flowers. I need to think about something besides this damn computer."

"What's it doing?"

"Nothing! It's eaten all my files. No correspondence, no bookkeeping, no e-mail. All gone. But I'm sure Jack can find everything. How do you take your coffee?"

"Black. Did you and the Denhams have any problem getting home yesterday?"

"No. We probably beat you, since you had to swing through Holland with Margaret Van Meter. Did you know she went to high school with Julie?"

"I learned it yesterday. I was surprised that Julie wasn't sent away to some fancy boarding school."

"That's what I would have expected, too. But Margaret told me they both went to Holland Christian Conservatives."

Actually, I don't know if Holland Christian High is conservative or not, but it has that reputation. Certainly Holland is a conservative community, and Holland Christian high school is associated with the Reformed Church, in the minds of the community, if not legally. Carolyn and I both nodded.

I expected Carolyn to ask about Mercy's flowers next, and I started to trot out the request I'd thought out, the one that I was sure I could say without getting my tongue tangled. But she fooled me. She handed me my coffee, leaned casually on the counter and said, "Actually, knowing Martin Schrader as intimately as I once did, I find it hard to believe Julie was sent to a religious high school."

As I say, she caught me completely off guard. My tongue took off of its own volition. At least, I'm sure my brain didn't tell it to say what came out.

"Martini Schizo seemed to be garnishing his mother," I said.

Carolyn and I stared at each other—she looked amazed, and I probably looked completely gaga. Then she laughed.

So I laughed, too. "I'm sorry, Carolyn," I said. " washed my tongue, and I can't do a thing with it. meant, after the funeral, Martin Schrader seemed to be intent on guarding his mother."

Carolyn was still laughing. "Lee, forgive me," she said. "I got all set to be totally cool about Martin Schrader, and you . . ." She quit talking and began laughing again.

I couldn't be offended. "As you can guess from my twisted tongue, I had a minor run-in with Martin Schrader and with his nephew. It's on my mind. And, yes, I had heard that you formerly dated Martin, and I was determined not to mention him to you."

Carolyn took a tissue from her pocket and blotted her eyes. "Actually, I think that's the first time I ever laughed about Martin. I feel much better for it. What happened to you?"

I quickly outlined Martin's request and the warning from Brad that followed it.

Carolyn went right to the heart of the problem. "You can hardly refuse to talk to a grieving uncle— if that's what Martin is—about his murdered niece," she said.

"I know. Of course, I'm not worried about meeting Martin, since I wouldn't meet anyone I don't know very well anyplace except my office. Or maybe a restaurant. I was more interested in Brad's comment. Is it true? Is Martin a 'dirty old man'? Or is that Brad's idea?"

"I think Brad's a callow youth," Carolyn said. "He's still young enough to be shocked by the thought of anyone over forty having sex. Martin is a chaser—as I found out the hard way—but 'dirty old man' is going too far. I don't think you need to take too many precautions if he wants to talk."

Still giggling now and then, Carolyn and I agreed on some flowers for Mercy Woodyard's birthday, and she called her supplier to make sure our selection—bronze roses—would be available. While she was on the phone there at the sales desk, I could hear a voice muttering swear words in her office, where Jack Ingersoll was still working. Carolyn had just confirmed my order and offered me a bill to deliver to Joe when Jack opened the office door and looked out.

"Carolyn! Have you checked all your windows?"

"That's what I've got you here to do, Jack. My Windows could be completely missing and I wouldn't know it."

Jack shook his head vigorously. "No, not Windows! Windows! Lowercase 'w,' not capital. The windows to your shop!"

"What do you mean?"

"As near as I can tell, there's nothing wrong with your computer or any of its programs."

"Then where did all my records go?"

"All I can figure is that someone got in, opened your computer, and erased everything in it."

Chapter 7

Jack came out of the office, all hair and snow boots, looking more like a mountain man than a computer nerd. "I'll swear there's not a thing wrong with your computer, Carolyn. I think somebody erased everything. Who's been fooling with it?"

"Nobody! Nobody's touched it but me."

"That's hard to believe. Could anybody have accessed your files without your knowing?"

"I don't see how."

"Was anybody suspicious in the shop late yesterday?"

"In January? In Warner Pier? I didn't even open up yesterday. And Lee's my first real, live customer today. Nobody could have gone into the office without my noticing."

Jack scratched his head. "Back to my first idea. You could have had a burglar."

Carolyn and I both laughed. "Why?" she said. "What would a burglar want here? I don't keep money here overnight, and I haven't begun to restock for the summer season. There's nothing here a burglar would want. Unless it was that computer. And it's still here."

"You better check your windows. Somebody's been messing with that computer, and if they didn't get at it while you were here, they must have done it while you weren't."

Carolyn was still scoffing, but she began to go from room to room, checking inside, and Jack took a look outside. In less than a minute, he put his head in through the back door and called out. "Look at the corner window!"

My curiosity was thoroughly aroused, so I followed Carolyn into a workroom. The window Jack wanted checked was over a large stainless steel sink. Anybody coming in or going out that window would have had to step into the sink.

"Don't touch anything," I said. "If somebody did get in, there might be fingerprints."

"I can't believe anybody burglarized the place," Carolyn said. "But I will say I don't usually leave the sink quite that dirty."

I peeked over her shoulder and looked into the bottom of the sink. There was dirt there, but—heck, this was a florist's shop. Flowers have roots, and roots are often buried in dirt.

"It doesn't look like footprints," I said.

Carolyn picked up a white ballpoint pen from the counter and used it to point to the window's standard, thumb-operated latch. "It's unlocked," she said. "But—hells bells! I'm not careful about keeping things locked. Not in the winter!"

I understood what she meant. It's a folk belief around Warner Pier. We're all convinced the summer people and tourists take all the crime home with them on Columbus Day. We seem to feel that Warner Pier is a Michigan version of Brigadoon; after the outsiders leave we lapse into a state of small town innocence until outsiders reappear the next June.

Jack was back inside by then. "Somebody's been stomping around in the snow under that window," he said. "I couldn't see any recognizable tracks, but maybe you'd better call the police."

Then he looked at his watch. "Your computer is up and running. I'll have to get into the hard drive to try to find out if anything can be salvaged. And I'll be glad to talk to the chief—or whoever he sends—about the break-in, but right now I'm going to run out to Hideaway Inn. Diane and Ronnie Denham have some kind of problem, too."

The Denhams had computer problems, too? That news gave me a severe case of jumping stomach—that queasy, upset feeling when my innards bounce around, up in the throat one minute and down in the toes the next.

What if Jack was wrong? What if Carolyn hadn't had a break-in? What if she had some sort of computer virus that destroyed all her files?

She and I exchanged e-mail daily. If she had a virus, I could, too.

Carolyn was calling 9-1-1, but I decided the Warner Pier police could investigate a possible burglary without me. I drove back to TenHuis Chocolade as quickly as possible. I almost skidded into the curb when I pulled up in front of the shop, and I did skid on the sidewalk as I ran toward the door. I opened my computer before I took my coat off, and as soon as it loaded I began opening files. I felt a surge of relief when I saw everything was there. Correspondence. Orders. Accounts receivable. E-mail. All the files I ordinarily use. Safe.

"Whew." My tummy settled into its normal place behind my navel. Then I got out a disk and backed up everything in all my business files right that minute.

While the computer was humming and clicking over that job, the door to the shop opened, and Jason came in.

He came directly into my office, and he didn't

mess around with small talk. "Listen, Lee, you've got a dial-up Internet connection with WarCo, don't you?"

"Yes. Why?"

"Don't connect, whatever you do. I got a virus that ate my whole system. I talked to WarCo, and they said it seemed to have come in by e-mail. Don't connect until you check with them, okay?"

I may have gasped. "Oh, no! The Denhams have computer problems, too, Jason, and so has Carolyn Rose."

"Do they have direct lines?"

"I don't know about the Denhams, but I don't think Carolyn does. She said that when she opened her computer this morning everything was gone. But Jack Ingersoll doesn't think it was a virus. He thinks somebody actually broke into her shop and erased everything in her computer."

"Weird!"

"It certainly is. I just backed up all my business files, but I haven't connected to WarCo yet. Thanks for the tip-off."

I agreed to call Margaret, and Jason said he'd talk to Lindy and Mike Herrera. Then Jason left.

Margaret answered on the first ring, and I was greatly relieved to hear that she hadn't had any computer troubles.

Margaret said her husband, Jim, was taking computer classes at the vo-tech school. "He knows what a dunce I am," she said, "so he set me up with a program that lets me keep my e-mail online. I never download anything. If I need a record, I just print it out. So if I have a virus, it's the server's problem, not mine. I don't use this computer for anything but e-mail and a record of orders and payments. And to print up bills. It does help at tax time. But mostly the kids use it to play games."

I called Lindy to make sure Jason had caught her.

She had her laptop with her. Its files were fine, she said.

"I took the day off, because I've got to work tonight," she said. "Mike has city council meeting, of course, and he wants me to be at Herrera's to close tonight." Herrera's is Mike's upscale restaurant. He keeps it and the Sidewalk Café open most of the winter. In addition to her catering job, Lindy fills in whenever he needs her at one of the restaurants.

Lindy promised to back up her files, and I hung up, relieved to find that not everyone in the Seventh Major Food Group seemed to have been hit by either a burglary or a computer virus.

By then the computer had finished copying the files I was most concerned about, and I took the disk out, marked it with "backup" and the date, then put it in my desk drawer. I resolved to think about something else. I hung my jacket on the coat tree in the corner, traded my snow boots for a pair of loafers, and wandered back into the shop, taking deep, soothing breaths laden with chocolate aroma. Aunt Nettie wasn't in sight, but the place was bustling, just the way a chocolate business should be four weeks before Valentine's Day.

I stopped beside Dolly Jolly, one of our newer employees. Dolly had popped up in our lives the previous summer, when she rented a remote cottage near Warner Pier to use as a retreat while she wrote a cookbook. When fall came, she decided she wanted to stay in Warner Pier. She rented the apartment over TenHuis Chocolade, and she asked for a chance to learn the chocolate business.

Dolly is unforgettable. She's taller than I am, built like a University of Michigan linebacker, and has brilliant red hair and a matching freckled face. And she can only speak at one decibel level—the top of her voice.

"Hi, Lee!" she shouted. At the same time she

flipped a five-inch mold over and gently tapped until what looked like a bowl of dark chocolate—actually a puffed, hollow heart—fell gently onto a metal tray, where it lay beside identical hearts.

"Hi, Dolly. How's the stock holding out?"

"Fine! But you might want to ask Nettie! She said something about needing raspberries!" Frozen raspberries are used to make the filling for a popular TenHuis bonbon.

I nodded. "We don't want to run out of raspberry creams." Because of their lovely pink insides and their yummy flavor, raspberry creams ("Red raspberry puree blended into a white chocolate cream interior, covered in dark chocolate") are highly popular at Valentine's. "Where's Aunt Nettie?"

Dolly pulled over a second tray, loaded with small solid chocolate hearts, cupids, and arrows. She began to fill the bigger hearts with an assortment of the small items. "She's in the break room working on something! Did you see the messages I left for you?"

"I guess not."

Dolly shrugged. "There were only a couple of calls! They said they'd call back! But this one guy came by!"

"Did he leave a name?"

"I left it on the desk! Martin? Martin something!"

I thought a moment. "Martin Schrader?"

"Older guy? Kinda short?"

Of course, to Dolly anybody who isn't playing in the NBA is "kinda short." But at not quite six feet, I'd looked down slightly when I talked to Martin Schrader face to face.

"Beautiful head of white hair?" I said.

Dolly nodded. I stood by and watched as she took a second five-inch dark chocolate heart, spread melted dark chocolate around its edge, then "glued" the two hollow hearts together. The most obvious result was a puffed, dark chocolate heart filled with special little Valentine symbols in dark, milk, and white chocolate. The second result would be a profit for TenHuis Chocolade; these were popular with our customers. Dolly used a spatula expertly, trimming away any chocolate that oozed out from the seam.

"Beautiful job," I said. "Aunt Nettie's sure happy that you wanted to come to work here." Dolly's face turned a shade brighter than usual, and I went on back to the break room. I found Aunt Nettie sitting at a table, hunched over a yellow legal pad.

She looked up and frowned. "I wish you could write this letter for me, Lee."

"You usually make me write all your letters. Why can't I write this one?"

"It's to Corrine."

I sat down across from Aunt Nettie. "Yes, you need to answer her yourself."

"If only I knew what to tell her about Bobby."

"You could just treat it like any other application, I guess. Tell Corrine all we have open is a routine clerical job or something like you've got Dolly doing—a sort of apprenticeship in how to make chocolate."

"Yes, I could do that. Then I'd ask for a résumé."

"If Bobby's interested."

"If he's interested."

I took a minute to tell Aunt Nettie about the computer problems that had hit Jason, House of Roses, and Hideaway Inn. Then I went back to my desk, feeling a little bit angry, a little bit fearful, and a little bit jealous. After all, Bobby was a blood relative to Aunt Nettie. I wasn't. As a matter of fact, he was probably her closest relation. If she were to fall into a vat of chocolate and drown that afternoon, Bobby could well get everything. I didn't even know if Aunt Nettie had a will or not. I could be working for Bobby and living in Bobby's house, the one *my* great-grandfather had built with his own hands.

Again Rachel Schrader's voice echoed in my subconscious. "I suppose you are your aunt's heir."

I sat down in my chair and slammed a desk drawer. Stupid! I was acting stupid! I'd only worked for TenHuis Chocolade a year and a half. Aunt Nettie had made chocolates for thirty-five years. The business belonged to her. She could do anything she pleased with it.

I stared at my computer screen and tried to think about something else. Anything else. E-mail. I called WarCo—our local server here in Warner County. They said they had identified the virus that hit Jason, and sure enough, a copy had also gone to me.

"What!" Fear gripped me.

"We got it stopped. It came from a fake address."

"How can you tell?"

"Easy. This one is pretty notorious. It was originally used by a guy who was a regular ecoterrorist."

"A what?"

"He claimed to be a supporter of ecology, only he did it by sending viruses to companies he thought didn't use ecological principles he approved of. They caught him finally."

"I hope they sent him up for life."

"No such luck. Anyway, the scuttlebutt is that he managed to convince the authorities he was only a tool of the organization he worked for. It may have been true. He got off with a big fine and a severe warning, but no jail time."

"Why would he want to attack the Seventh Food Group?"

"Oh, I don't think it's the same guy. I think someone has appropriated one of their addresses. Everybody in the trade knew the addresses."

Assured that my e-mail was safe, I opened it up. There were a dozen orders and queries. For the next forty-five minutes I concentrated on clearing them out. I replied to the queries, attaching my stored price list to several of them. I acknowledged the orders and moved them out of the e-mail file and into a special file I keep for those. I printed out a note from my mother, detailing her itinerary for a trip to Brazil, then hit REPLY and sent a message urging her to have fun. I didn't go into my personal problems with her.

I had no other personal e-mail besides that one message from my mom. For a moment I missed Julie's annoying jokes and inspirational items.

By the time I had finished handling e-mail, I was in a much better frame of mind. I might still be jealous and suspicious of Bobby, but I felt calmer and more confident in Aunt Nettie's ability to handle her own affairs.

And I was thinking about computers, so the problems that had hit the Seventh Major Food Group came back to mind. I gave in to curiosity and called Diane Denham to find out about the electronic woes at the Hideaway Inn.

Diane sounded dispirited. "I'm really upset over this virus," she said.

"Then you got hit by the same virus that hit Jason?"

"That's what Jack Ingersoll thinks. Our files are gone, Lee! Kaput! Zip! All our reservations for next summer. All our accounts. All our correspondence. Gone! Why would anyone do this?"

I didn't have an answer, so I listened sympathetically until Diane was ready to hang up. Then I tried vainly to work on my own business. But it was no go. I simply couldn't concentrate. Finally, I went back to the shop and found Aunt Nettie.

"I give up," I said. "I'll have to work late tonight."

"Why? What's wrong?"

"Nothing's wrong with the business. I just can't get these computer problems out of my mind. It's nearly time for Tracy to come in for her after-school gig on the counter. I'm going back to House of Roses and see if the police found out anything."

Aunt Nettie smiled. "If you're not going home for dinner, maybe you and I could snatch a pizza. Whenever you're ready."

"That'll be fun. You and I don't eat dinner together—just the two of us—very often these days. Since your social life is so active."

I left Aunt Nettie smiling, put on all my winter regalia, and went back to House of Roses. When I went in the shop's front door, Carolyn looked out of her office.

"I don't see any crime scene tape," I said. "Have the police been here?"

"Chief Jones came himself."

"I think he does all the detective work." Warner Pier has only four guys on the force, after all.

"He certainly acts as if he knows what's what when it comes to a crime scene. And he thought Jack was right. He found scratches on that window. Plus, he thought somebody had deliberately messed up the tracks outside the window—you know, so they couldn't be identified. But he said it would be hard to catch the burglar."

I followed Carolyn into her office. "When does Jack think he can work on your hard drive?"

"Not for a week or more. He's got to do a job in Holland. Some insurance office. He said he could come in the evening, but I don't want to hang around here all day waiting for customers and all night keeping Jack company."

Carolyn reached for her telephone pad. "By the way, I got confirmation on the roses for Joe's mother. The bronze variety is available."

"Good. The rust and cream colors ought to look good in her office. Did they confirm the price? I'd better write it down."

Carolyn looked through some papers on her desk. "The price is right here. Someplace."

I picked up a notepad Carolyn had placed at a spot that would be handy for customers, then reached for a ballpoint pen. On the corner of the desk was a brass jug full of the rainbow-hued ones she passed out to customers. And right in the middle of twenty-five rainbow-hued pens was one white one.

Carolyn picked up a slip of paper and turned back toward me. "Help yourself to a pen," she said. "I'm trying to get rid of those."

"Are you changing your logo?" I said. "That white pen is really different."

"White pen?" Carolyn frowned, then focused her eyes on the brass vase and its contents. "Where did that come from?"

She picked it up and turned it over, looking at it closely.

I could see the light dawn. She might as well have yelled, "Eureka!"

"What is it?" I asked.

Carolyn gave a sly smile, then chuckled. "It's nothing. I just remembered where this pen came from." She stuck the pen in her center desk drawer, then smiled at me. Her whole mood seemed to have changed. She'd been depressed. Now she was elated.

"I'll have Mercy's roses out by noon tomorrow," she said. And she actually hummed a little tune.

I was going to ask just what had changed her outlook, but her phone rang. Carolyn answered it. "Sure, Lee's here," she said. Then she handed me the receiver.

It was Tracy, the high school girl who was helping us with retail sales every afternoon during the Valentine rush.

"Lee?" Her voice was low. "There's a guy here to see you. A Mr. Schrader. He says it's important."

Rats. As soon as I'd left the office, Martin Schrader had come back. I sighed and decided I might as well get the meeting with him over.

"Okay," I said. "Tell him to wait in my office. I'll be right there."

I told Carolyn I had a minor emergency at the office and drove back to TenHuis Chocolade. As I entered the shop, Tracy beckoned to me. "I almost never got that guy to sit down in your office," she said. "He kept roaming around the shop."

"He's probably just nervous, Tracy. He's the uncle of that girl who was murdered in Holland. I'm sure the whole family is upset."

"He's her uncle? He doesn't look old enough to be anybody's uncle."

I turned and looked through the glass wall that surrounded my little cubbyhole of an office. I expected to see the distinguished and handsome gray-haired Martin Schrader.

But instead I saw a skinny, dark-haired guy with a hangdog expression.

My caller was not Martin Schrader. It was his nephew, Brad.

Chapter 8

My first reaction was annoyance. I'd cut short my questions for Carolyn because I felt obligated to talk to Martin Schrader. And my visitor turned out to be his nerdy nephew. I wouldn't have hesitated to let Brad sit an hour. After all, he hadn't even hinted that he was going to drop by.

My second reaction was a major itch on my curiosity bump. Why had Brad come?

Common politeness required that I find out; so did extreme nosiness. I went into the office, shook hands with Brad, and sat down at my desk.

"I didn't expect to see you again so soon," I said. "What brings you by?"

Brad's voice squeaked as much today as it had the day before. "I guess I wanted to ask your advice." Brad dropped his head and stared at the floor. "I was wondering what was the best way to get acquainted in Warner Pier. You know, meet people."

I was astonished. "Let's back up here, Brad. I didn't even know you lived in Warner Pier."

"I don't exactly. I live a mile north, in a little house

on my grandmother's property. It's always been called 'the cabin.' I drive to Grand Rapids to work."

"You work for Schrader Laboratories?"

"Yeah. Uncle Marty thought I should try to learn something about the family firm." Brad's voice held an undertone of sarcasm on the two final words, but his eyes didn't match it. They took on a whipped-puppy look. Then he spoke again. "Julie told me you'd only been here a few years, but you seemed to know everybody in Warner Pier. I guess I thought you might have a magic method of getting to know people."

All of a sudden my heart went out to Brad. He was such a nerd, with an annoying voice and an insecure manner. Which didn't mean he wasn't a nice guy. But he must have always had trouble making friends because of his unfortunate mannerisms.

"I don't know that there's any magic trick you can use to get acquainted in a new community, Brad. If I managed it in Warner Pier, it's because I work for my aunt, and everybody in town knows her. So they all have to be nice to me. Plus, I'd worked here summers when I was in high school, and I got to be friends with Lindy Herrera back then. She's introduced me around, too. And after I started dating Joe Woodyard, the guy I'm planning to marry, he introduced me to his friends. So I may have been a stranger in Warner Pier, but I had a lot of local connections."

Brad was looking even more downhearted. Obviously, he didn't have local connections.

I tried to think of something encouraging to suggest. "I did do a couple of things on my own, though. I made an effort to meet people I thought I'd have something in common with. My banker, for example. We're both interested in getting ahead in business. I went down to her office the first time we needed to talk, and I enjoyed meeting her. So, the next week, I called and asked her to go to lunch. We've become really good friends. She suggested that I sign up for a chamber of commerce committee, and I jumped at it." I laughed. "I think any community will warm up to a willing horse."

"A willing horse?"

"You know the old saying, 'Work a willing horse to death.' Find some activity you're interested in. And volunteer."

"I support the Lake Michigan Conservation Society."

"Great! They should have a lot of things going on—cleaning beaches? You'll have to get out and do the grunt work, of course. Sweep floors. Wash dishes."

"They don't seem to have projects like that. It's mainly lobbying."

"Then find some organization that does need manual labor. If you're interested in ecology—"

"I am! Sort of."

"There are other groups around that need workers. Pretty soon you'll discover you know people. You'll be running into them at the Superette. If I did anything active to get acquainted in Warner Pier, that was it."

Brad still looked doubtful. "But you've got an edge. You're really pretty."

"There's nothing wrong with your looks, Brad." That was true, I realized. Brad didn't *look* odd; he *acted* odd.

"Appearance may attract people on a superficial level," I said, "but real, true friends aren't concerned about your looks. Being friendly and cheerful is a lot more attractive than physical beauty."

Brad gave me a sly look out of the corner of his eye, but he didn't say anything. If he had, I knew what it would have been—"Easy for you to say." I decided there was no point in telling Brad I'd ruined years of my life worrying about my looks because my mother thought they were important.

"But you've got that cute Texas accent," he said.

"Don't tell me that! I worked with a speech coach three years trying to get rid of that cute Texas accent."

"It's better than my New York one."

I gave my widest grin. "You can always offer people a cuppa 'kwaffee.' That sounds pretty cute."

Brad finally smiled back. "How about the other people Julie knew here in Warner Pier? Are all of them natives?"

"Lindy is. But Carolyn Rose just came here a few years ago. I think the Denhams bought Hideaway Inn after Diane took early retirement. They haven't been here long."

"What about the others on the list?"

"I don't know if Jason's a native, but he's lived here a long time. And Margaret grew up in Holland. In fact, she went to Holland Christian with Julie."

"Yeah, Julie told me they knew each other in high school."

I was getting tired of being quizzed by Brad. Maybe I could find out a few things about Julie if I turned the tables and began questioning him.

"Didn't Julie ever introduce you to any of her friends in Holland?"

"Oh, she wanted to, but it never worked out. Tell me about Mrs. Herrera. She's with Herrera Catering? Where is that?"

"Their offices are right down the street, over the Sidewalk Café. But Lindy's not there much."

"Does she work from home?"

"Sometimes. Her job is special assistant for her father-in-law, Mike Herrera. She fills in wherever he needs her. Like tonight, she's in charge of Herrera's, their upscale restaurant."

I tried to turn the conversation back to Julie. "You

know, Brad, all of us in the Food Group thought that Julie must have a boyfriend. She was a darling girl. But she never mentioned anybody special in her e-mail, and we didn't spot anybody at the memorial service who seemed to be a likely candidate."

"She hadn't been dating anybody seriously that I knew about."

"I can't believe Julie didn't have an active social life. Would your uncle know anything about it?"

Brad shrugged. "I think Uncle Martin kept trying to introduce her to guys in Grand Rapids. You know, doctors and lawyers and executives." Again I caught that slight sarcasm when Brad referred to his uncle. Or was it the reference to business, as in "executives"?

"I guess I can ask your uncle," I said.

"Ask him? About Julie?"

"Yes. He's supposedly coming by here this afternoon."

I glanced at my watch, and as I did I caught a swift movement out of the corner of my eye. When I looked back at Brad, he was standing up. The movement had been Brad. He had leaped to his feet like a jackrabbit with a coyote after him.

"I've bothered you long enough," he said. "Please don't tell Uncle Martin I came by." He was moving out of the office.

I stood up, too. "You can't leave without a sample of TenHuis chocolate."

"Oh, you don't need to give me candy." By now he was out of the office and in the middle of our little retail shop.

I followed him. "It's not 'candy,' Brad. It's chocolate. Quite a different thing. Come on now. You'll hurt my feelings if you don't have a sample. What do you like? Dark chocolate or milk chocolate?"

Brad kept edging toward the door. "Dark, I guess."

"Okay, how about Jamaican rum? Our sales mate-

rial calls it 'the ultimate dark chocolate truffle.' Or
a double fudge bonbon? 'Layers of milk and dark
chocolate fudge, enrobed in dark chocolate.' "

"Either one!" Tracy, who had been listening to all
this, opened the glass showcase, took out a Jamaican
rum truffle in a pleated paper cup, and held it out
to Brad. He pulled a stocking cap down over his ears,
took the truffle, and stood there looking at it.

Then he turned back to me. "About Julie and her
love life—actually, I think she'd been afraid to date
since her marriage broke up."

"Her marriage? Julie had been married?"

Brad nodded and waved his Jamaican rum truffle
at me. "Thanks," he said. Then he scampered out the
door before I could say anything more than, "Brad!"

He went off up the street, almost running, though
he did pop his truffle into his mouth while I could
still see him through our big window.

"What a weird guy!" Tracy said.

I guess I answered her, but I was thinking about
the stunning announcement Brad had made as he
left. Julie had been married? She'd never mentioned
it. But Julie had never mentioned anything about herself. She had concentrated on learning all about other
people, but her own ideas, needs, desires, and history
had been a deep secret.

Who had Julie married? What had happened to the
marriage? "Her marriage broke up," Brad had said.
Had she been divorced? Separated? Was she still
married? Was her husband her heir? Did the Holland
cops know that he existed?

Tracy spoke again. "Actually, if you got that Brad
Schrader guy on one of these redo shows—you
know, got him a new wardrobe, a new haircut, and
taught him how to talk . . ."

"Then he wouldn't be the same person," I said. My
voice was sharp. Where did Tracy get off criticizing
Brad? She was no glamour girl herself, though she had

smartened up a bit in the past few months. I reminded myself that she was just a high school kid, and I forced my voice to be softer. "Brad's a nerd, but that doesn't mean he isn't a nice guy, Tracy."

I went back to my office feeling more sorry for Brad than ever. He had run away because he didn't want to meet his uncle and had asked me not to tell his uncle he'd come by. Every time there had been the slightest reference to Martin Schrader, Brad had displayed an uneasy attitude. Was Martin Schrader trying to be a mentor to Brad? Did Brad resent it? Or were they battling over something? What about Brad's father and mother?

Brad had given me a lot to think about, and the most important thing was the news he had dropped about Julie. She'd been married. I eyed my computer and thought about going on the Internet to check out the wedding stories in the *Grand Rapids Press* back issues. But I didn't even know if Julie had been married in Grand Rapids. Or in Holland. Or in Michigan. Though I'd expect a Schrader wedding anywhere would be news for the *Grand Rapids Press*.

I was dying to talk to somebody about this. To Lindy. The very person. I reached for the phone, then looked at my watch. It was nearly five o'clock. Lindy would be busy at Herrera's, getting ready to open. I couldn't bother her with a tidbit of gossip, no matter how fascinating.

I decided I'd better simply get back to work. Maybe Martin Schrader would show up yet that afternoon, and I'd ask him about Julie's marriage. I turned to my computer and thought chocolate.

I checked my e-mail again, sorted a couple of new messages into the right electronic files, then began handling orders. At five thirty Aunt Nettie came in and said she had to run a few errands in Holland. "Do you mind putting our dinner excursion off until I get back?" she said.

"Not a bit." I opened my desk drawer. "I have my trusty stash of Amaretto and Dutch caramel."

She laughed and left. Each TenHuis employee is allowed two chocolates each day—truffles, bonbons, or molded solids. We're supposed to stay out of the fancy molded items, such as the puffed heart filled with tiny chocolates that Dolly Jolly had been working on earlier. Amaretto truffles, Irish Cream bonbons, and Dutch caramel bonbons are my favorites. I snag a couple from the counter every morning, and if I don't eat both during the day, I leave the uneaten ones in my drawer. Lots of days I can't find time to relish prime chocolates, so I often save up a stash of a half dozen or so.

I ate a Dutch caramel—these have soft and creamy insides, nothing like the stuff used to make caramel apples—and went back to work. But in the back of my mind I was still thinking about Julie, about the startling news Brad had given me, and about how much I wanted to talk to Lindy about it. I guess that was the reason, after Aunt Nettie got back from Holland, that I suggested we skip the pizza and go to Herrera's for dinner.

"Herrera's?" Aunt Nettie looked down at her white pants and tunic, topped by a blue sweater. "I'm not very dressed up."

"This is Warner Pier. Nobody dresses up."

"But there's a difference between designer sportswear and a food service uniform."

"I thought a nice dinner would be a little treat for us. I've got room on my MasterCard."

"You've convinced me."

So, at seven forty-five p.m. Aunt Nettie and I parked in front of Herrera's, went in and were warmly greeted by Lindy, who was acting as hostess.

Herrera's is down on the water; a great location in the summertime, when the tourists and summer people fill every table and form a line outside. The main room is large and paneled in limed oak, with large-scale landscapes by local artists. In the summer these emphasize pastel colors.

In the winter, when the view of the frozen river turns off any desire for iced tea or jellied consommé, the room's fancy plantation shutters are firmly closed. Mike makes a few other changes to make the place feel warmer—red velvet draperies replace the white linen ones he uses in spring and summer, the candles on each table are larger than the votives used in warmer weather, and the pale landscapes are replaced by equally large-scale ones in darker tones.

But it's still an impressive ambience. The service is impressive, too. Lindy sent over a bottle of wine, and the wine steward popped the cork and filled our glasses before we could do more than glance at the menu. He draped the bottle with a napkin and put it on the corner of the table.

Aunt Nettie ordered chicken Cordon Bleu—Herrera's version is not prepackaged—and I went for the pork loin with tart cherry sauce. We both ordered soup and skipped salad.

I'd told Lindy I had a piece of hot gossip for her, so she joined us just as the soup was served. She was as astonished as I was to learn that Julie had been married.

"It must not have been while she was living in Holland," she said. "She sure never gave a hint."

"Margaret will know."

"Probably. But she's never given a hint either."

"How about Jason?"

Lindy stood up. "I'll check on the kitchen. Then I'll call him."

"Honestly," Aunt Nettie said. She smiled, but she was scolding me, too. "Poor Julie is dead. Does it matter if she had been married or not?"

I ate soup and thought about it. Was I simply being nosy? I ate three spoonfuls of soup while I came up with the answer.

"I don't think our interest in Julie's marriage is merely nosiness," I said. "Not in the gossipy sense, anyway. I think it's guilt. Julie was the focal point of our little e-mail group, the one who kept it going. She did all of us some favors on the business front, and she made an effort to be friendly to all of us. She dropped in on Margaret, who's pretty housebound with those six kids. She came down to Warner Pier and took Lindy and Carolyn and me to lunch. She sent the Denhams some business, I know.

"But when she died, I realized that none of us knew anything about her. We hadn't even known she'd been married! I know Julie and I weren't close friends, but it makes me feel bad because I took her for granted while she was alive."

Aunt Nettie's smile was good-humored. "As long as you don't think you have to get involved in the investigation of her death, Lee."

"Oh, no! I've been down that road before, and I had to buy a new van to prove it! Any more murders, and they're gonna cancel my insurance."

We both laughed and settled back to enjoy our dinner. But way in the back of my mind, a few thoughts did bubble up. The Holland police thought Julie had been killed by a burglar. That burglar had stolen—among other things—her computer. Jack Ingersoll thought House of Roses had had a burglar. A burglar who did nothing but destroy Carolyn's computer records. Jason and the Hideaway Inn had been hit by a vicious computer virus. Could these things be connected?

If anything happened to my computer, I might get pulled into the investigation of Julie's death whether I wanted to be or not.

When Aunt Nettie and I had finished dinner,

Lindy came over to say she had talked to Jason, and he hadn't known anything about Julie's marriage. But he was going to call someone who might know, then call her back. Aunt Nettie went on home, but Lindy brought a pot of coffee, and I lingered while the Herrera's crew cleaned up. She finally got around to telling me that her e-mail had been attacked by the same virus that hit mine, but our local computer server, WarCo, had been able to stop it before she connected. Another narrow escape.

Ten o'clock came, the last customer had gone, the kitchen was cleaned, and Lindy had packed up her laptop. Still no word from Jason.

"I don't think he'll call this late," Lindy said. "I've let everybody out the back."

"I'm parked out front," I said. "If you'll let me out that way, I'll be gone."

"It's been nice to have company."

The stars were bright as I crossed the sidewalk. I could see the lights of the town glinting off the ice in the river. I paused to look at the view, then realized Lindy was standing at the door, waiting for me to get into my van safely. I did so, checking behind the seats and in the rear deck. Okay, I admit it; Julie's death had made me jumpy.

Well, I thought, if Lindy can watch and make sure I'm safe, I'd better do the same for her. I knew she was parked in the alley, so I warmed the van up for a minute, backed it out, then drove down the street and turned the corner. Halfway down the block I swung into the alley. My lights hit Lindy's compact car.

It took me a moment to register the two figures beside the car.

One figure was on the ground, lying terribly still, and the second held something that looked like a club.

CHOCOLATE CHAT

CHOCOLATE THROUGH THE AGES

(Describing the first view of cocoa beans by Europeans) "They seemed to hold these almonds at a great price; for when they were brought on board ship together with their goods, I observed that when any of these almonds fell, they all stooped to pick it up, as if an eye had fallen."
—Fernand Columbus, recorded in 1502, during the fourth voyage of his father, Christopher Columbus

"If you are not feeling well, if you have not slept, chocolate will revive you. But you have no chocolate pot! I think of that again and again! My dear, how will you ever manage?"
—Marquise de Sévigné, 1677, quoted by Sophie D. Coe and Michael D. Coe in *The True History of Chocolate*

"The superiority of chocolate, both for health and nourishment, will soon give it the same preference over tea and coffee in America which it has in Spain."
—Thomas Jefferson

Chapter 9

I hit the horn and held it down. I guess I was yelling, too. And I slipped the van into neutral and gunned it. Don't ask me why. I guess I just wanted to make a lot of noise.

All this commotion got results. The guy dropped the club and clutched something to his chest, then jumped up and ran.

I stopped with my fist still on the horn. Now I could see that the figure on the ground was Lindy. Or at least it had a red cap like Lindy's and was wearing Lindy's blue down coat. This did not surprise me, since I'd been expecting to see Lindy in that alley.

I had finally acquired a cell phone, and luckily, it was in my purse. I punched in 9-1-1 as I hopped out of the van, then knelt beside Lindy in the headlights. She was breathing, thank God.

It seemed like hours before the Warner Pier patrol car got there. I stood over Lindy, clutching the cell phone and talking to the dispatcher, terrified that her attacker would come back. I was afraid to move her, but I pulled off my wool scarf and slid it under her cheek, which had been resting on the icy ground.

The Warner Pier EMTs, who are volunteers, were only a minute behind the cops. By the time they pulled into the alley, Lindy was groaning and stirring.

The next hour was confusing. Hogan Jones and Joe showed up just after the EMTs, both of them on foot. They'd still been at the city council meeting, and both had run the four blocks from City Hall since it was faster than getting into their cars.

Joe showed a satisfying relief that I wasn't hurt—the dispatcher had paged the chief and told him only that I'd called in a 9-1-1 report on an attack behind Herrera's. The chief had nudged Joe and told him I was in danger, and they had arrived with no more information than that. I guess it was lucky neither of them had a heart attack. Mike Herrera was close behind them, so I gathered that the city council meeting had adjourned abruptly.

Joe and Mike left almost immediately to tell Tony what had happened. Joe stayed at Tony and Lindy's to baby-sit the three Herrera kids so Tony could follow Lindy to the nearest hospital, thirty miles away in Holland. Mike came back to the alley to let the police into the restaurant and be available with other information they might need.

The chief asked me a lot of questions, but I didn't have many answers. I hadn't seen much.

The guy—or gal—who'd been standing over Lindy had worn standard west Michigan winter gear: a dark parka or ski jacket with a hood. The hood had been over the attacker's head. I hadn't been able to tell if the person was dark, light, fat, thin, or in between. He—or she—had run off at a crouch, so I couldn't even tell if the attacker was tall or short. The face had been a dark blob, which might have meant it was covered by a stocking mask or a ski mask. Or it might have simply meant the attacker kept his face out of my headlights. His jacket had had no distinctive features—no stripes, checks, or readable brand names.

A short piece of scrap wood was lying beside Lindy, and apparently this was the club I had seen the attacker raising. It was the kind of thing that might be found in any Dumpster in the alley. The chief and the patrolman looked for footprints, but the alley had been plowed, so the snow wasn't deep, and in the middle of a January night it was mostly ice anyway.

"I guess the guy is agile," I said. "I would have fallen down and broken my neck if I'd run off the way he did."

"We'll check in the daylight," Chief Jones said. "But I doubt we'll find anything."

Joe came back about then. Tony had alerted Lindy's mom and dad, and they'd arrived to watch over the sleeping kids. Tony had already called from the hospital with a preliminary report that Lindy was demanding to go home, so we were deducing that she was not seriously hurt.

"It must have been a thief," I said. "The guy ran off carrying something, and I don't see her purse anyplace."

"We'll have to ask Lindy just what she had on her," the chief said. "Joe, you follow Lee home."

He'd alerted Aunt Nettie, of course, so she insisted that Joe come in so she could comfort us with coffee and bonbons—crème de menthe ("The formal after-dinner mint") and Italian cherry ("Amarena cherry in syrup and white chocolate cream"). We sat around the dining room table, and I had to tell the whole story.

After I finished, Aunt Nettie shook her head in

disbelief. "It's hard to imagine that a thief would attack Lindy," she said. "It's not likely she would be carrying the night's take from Herrera's."

"I'll bet that ninety percent of Herrera's customers use credit cards," Joe said. "If you took the night's take from Herrera's, it probably would be less than fifty dollars in cash money and a whole lot of receipts. You're right. It doesn't sound like a thief."

"Then who was it?" I said. "A sex maniac? When the temperature is down in the teens? He *would* be a maniac. But it did appear that Lindy's purse was missing. At least, it wasn't in the car."

"Did she even have a purse?" Aunt Nettie said. "I've seen Lindy stuff her car keys in her pocket."

"I saw her pack her belongings up before I left," I said. I closed my eyes and tried to remember. "I didn't pay much attention. But you're right. She did stick her keys in her coat pocket. She had a little, flat envelope purse. And she put it in the zipper pocket on the side of her laptop case."

I gasped. "Golly! That's what was taken. Not her purse! Her laptop!"

Joe called the chief and told him to look for the laptop in the car and inside the restaurant.

After he hung up, he nodded at me. "I think you're right. Lindy never goes anyplace without that laptop."

"She wouldn't have left it at Herrera's," I said, "because she didn't work there every day. She would have taken it home."

I was sure that was right. Lindy's laptop—the computer she used to plan events for Herrera's Catering, the machine that handled her schedule, the gadget she used for her e-mail—it had gone down the alley with the formless figure who had attacked her.

And the computers of Jason, Carolyn Rose, and the Denhams had also been involved in weird events that day.

"This is the fourth time." I whispered the words.

"The fourth time for what?" Joe asked.

"It's the Seventh Major Food Group," I said. "Odd things are happening to all our computers."

He looked incredulous, and I realized I hadn't seen Joe all day. I hadn't had an opportunity to tell him about the damage to Jason's computer, to the Denhams' computer, to Carolyn Rose's. So I told him.

"But that's crazy," Joe said. "Everybody knows an expert can get that stuff back. All those political and Wall Street scandals have showed that to the public. Even if you try to erase everything on a computer, it's still on the hard drive someplace."

But I was convinced. "Maybe we're being attacked by a computer illiterate," I said. "I'm going to talk to the chief about it."

Aunt Nettie gave a big yawn at that point—it was after midnight—and we adjourned our meeting.

Joe kissed me good night, then headed for his truck. He called out one last bit of advice. "Keep your cell phone by your bed!"

"We won't have any problem," I said. "I don't have a computer here. I just hope nobody breaks into the shop."

I put on a flannel nightgown and piled all my extra blankets on top of my quilt. I was shaking, and it was probably nerves, not cold. I burrowed under all this weight of wool, acrylic, and cotton batting. I'd begun to feel warmer and was drifting off to sleep. A year from now, I thought, I'll be sleeping with Joe every night, and I'll stick these icy feet right on his back. After all, what are husbands for?

"Husbands." The word jolted me awake.

For a minute I didn't know why. Then I remembered the question that had occupied Lindy and me most of the evening.

Julie's husband? Who had he been? When and where had they gotten married? The attack on Lindy had completely distracted me from that question.

Chief Hogan Jones was a friend. I could ask him if the Holland police knew Julie had been married. I dropped off to sleep thinking that I had quite a lot to talk to him about.

I called his office first thing in the morning, but he wasn't there. Instead, he dropped by TenHuis Chocolade about ten a.m. It wasn't a very satisfactory visit. I might have had plenty to talk to Hogan about, but it turned out that he had even more to talk to me about.

He was mad when he walked in, and we got even further at odds when he seemed to interpret my information about Julie's marriage as an insult to law enforcement. He blew his stack.

"Of course the Holland police know Julie Singletree had been married!" It was the first time I'd ever heard Hogan yell. "That's the first question they ask!"

"Who did she marry?"

"I'm not telling you, Lee!"

"Why not?"

"Because you don't need to know."

"But Julie was a frog—I mean a friend! Julie was a friend of mine."

"If she was such a friend, why didn't she tell you about her marriage herself?"

He had me there. Recklessly disregarding the mood he was in, I tried another tack. "Are they looking at everyone's computers?"

"The Holland police are handling their own investigation. They haven't asked my advice. And they don't need yours!"

"But the Seventh Major Food Group—"

"Lee! Stay out of it!"

"Look, Hogan, two friends of mine have been attacked, and one of them was killed. Three others have had weird things happen to commuters. I mean computers! Am I supposed to ignore this?"

"You're supposed to be reasonable and leave it to

the police! I'm not talking to you about this any more!"

We might have left it at that and parted without any more yelling if Aunt Nettie hadn't joined in. She'd heard us, I guess, and she showed up at the office door. "Now just what are you two arguing about?"

Neither of us answered, so she smiled her sunny smile and spoke again. "Come now, surely you can both discuss your differences without yelling."

That was not the right thing to say to Hogan Jones right at that moment. He pointed a finger at me, but he spoke to Aunt Nettie. "You talk to her! She's going to get in trouble, nosing around where she has no business!"

I yelled back. "I'm just worried about my fiends! My friends!"

Aunt Nettie drew herself up with great dignity. "Hogan, if Lee is concerned about her friends, I hardly think that's a quality worthy of criticism."

"These are not close friends."

Aunt Nettie's voice was icy. "Lindy is."

"We're keeping an eye on Lindy. We're keeping an eye on everybody. But we may not be able to if Lee keeps stirring things up!"

"I don't believe Lee has 'stirred things up,' Hogan. She has merely had concerns for her fellow human beings, and she's acted on them. She hasn't interfered with law enforcement in any way. She's just trying to help her friends."

"These are not her friends!"

I got back into the fray at that point. "You keep telling me these people are not friends. But that's stupid, Hogan! We may not be buffet—I mean bosom! We may not be bosom buddies, but so what? I'm still convinced that strange things are happening to all of us. They may be in danger! I've got to do what I can to head that danger off."

"But you don't really know these people!"

"What does that matter? Even if they're complete strangers, I can't let something happen to them without trying to stop it!"

"You don't get it!"

"No, I don't! I don't understand why you don't want me to try to help them!" I stood up then and leaned across my desk. "Whether I know them well or not, they're my friends!"

Hogan leaned across the desk, too, and we stood there, practically nose to nose. And when he spoke again, his voice had become quiet. Too quiet.

"These are not friends," he said. "These are suspects."

Then he zipped up his jacket and left.

Chapter 10

Neither Aunt Nettie nor I spoke until Hogan was out the door.

"Oh, my," Aunt Nettie said. "I hadn't thought of it that way."

"Neither had I," I said.

I was relieved when she went back to the workroom, leaving me to think over Hogan's parting comment and to feel stupid on my own.

Well, naturally. From the viewpoint of law enforcement, if something was happening to the people in the Seventh Major Food Group and to their computers, the members of the group themselves would be the obvious suspects. After all, if there was something strange going on, who was most closely involved?

But could a member of the Seventh Major Food Group have actually killed Julie? The idea seemed ludicrous. None of us knew her well enough, for one thing. What possible motive could any of us have had for killing her? We all liked her. Or I thought we did. Of course, Carolyn had once called her "Little Miss Knows-All." But she hadn't dropped out of the newslist over it.

I tried to put the whole matter aside. And maybe I did, for an hour. But as lunchtime neared, I began to wonder how Lindy was doing. Finally, at eleven forty-five, I called. I told myself that if Lindy was in bed, her mother would be there to answer the phone. But Lindy answered on the first ring.

"Hi, Lindy. I hope I didn't get you up."

"No. The doctor said I should take it easy today, and Tony's enforcing his prescription. I'm going nuts sitting around here. I need someone to talk to."

"Do you want me to bring you some lunch?"

"Bring me a strawberry truffle, and I'll make grilled cheese sandwiches."

"Deal."

I loaded up a half-pound box of TenHuis's best—four of Lindy's favorite strawberry truffles ("White chocolate and strawberry interior coated with dark chocolate"), plus some solid hearts for the kids and four mocha pyramids ("Milky coffee interior shaped into a pyramid and enrobed with dark chocolate"). I knew Tony liked those.

I parked in Lindy's drive a few minutes after twelve. It was a bright, glary day. The sun glinted off the snow-covered yard and off the roofs of the houses in Lindy's neighborhood, making me grateful for my sunglasses. Lindy's sidewalk had been cleared, and she opened the front door as I stepped onto the porch. I didn't comment on the big bruise on her left temple.

"Sure is good to see a human face," Lindy said.

"I'm almost surprised that the chief is letting you stay alone. After all, somebody actually hit you in the head last night."

"It must have been a thief, Lee. Somebody too dumb to realize I wouldn't have any money on me."

Joe, Aunt Nettie, and I had demolished that theory

the night before, but I didn't argue. I noticed that Lindy carefully locked the door behind me and that she was wearing her cell phone on the belt of her jeans. She was obviously being cautious, and there was no point in my making her more nervous than she was.

We talked about home decor while Lindy grilled our sandwiches. She and Tony had bought the 100-year-old frame house a few months earlier, and they had a long list of do-it-yourself projects waiting for them. At the moment all the living room furniture was piled in the dining room because Tony had promised to paint that weekend, but there was plenty of room for their family to eat in what Aunt Nettie called the "breakfast nook." Some previous owner had added the built-in table and benches to the kitchen, maybe sometime in the 1940s.

We'd eaten our sandwiches and carrot sticks, and Lindy had opened the box of candy before either of us mentioned Julie.

"The chief came over and grilled me for half an hour this morning," she said. "He's afraid this business last night is connected to Julie's death."

"He came by the shop and lectured me. Told me to stop being so nosy."

"That's like telling your aunt to stop cooking, isn't it?"

"I'm afraid you're right. Nosiness is a basic part of my personality. But I'm trying to follow his recommendation. So you'll have to tell me what he wanted to know without my asking about it."

Lindy grinned. "The first part of it wasn't too surprising. He wanted to know if I remembered anything about last night. I don't. I remember closing the back door. Then I woke up in the ambulance."

"I think that's fairly typical, from what I've read about head injuries."

"I was lucky not to be hurt worse. The chief told

me the reason I was lucky was that you decided to drive around to the alley."

"No biggie. You'd waited at the front door of Herrera's to make sure I was in the van safely. It seemed as if I should return the favor."

Lindy gave a slight shudder, and I scrambled through my brain for a new topic to introduce. But Lindy spoke again before I could. "The main thing the chief was interested in, Lee, was the Seventh Major Food Group. He wanted to know all about the people in it. How well I knew them. What I thought of them. Of course, you're the only one I know very well."

"How about Jason?"

"We knew each other off and on the whole time he worked for Mike, but he tended bar, and I usually worked in the restaurants, so it wasn't a regular thing. Mike thinks a lot of him. But I will say that Jason is the only person I ever heard complain about Julie before she died."

"Did he hate her dumb jokes as much as I did?"

Lindy laughed. "You're the only one I heard complain about those—though I agreed with you! No, Jason had some other problem with her. He griped about her talking too much. He said her mouth was the size of a CNN satellite and broadcast just as widely."

"Oh, gee! She must have really blabbed something he didn't want mentioned."

"She did tend to do that. She told a couple of things I didn't really want mentioned. You remember, that day all of us had lunch? Julie, Carolyn, you, and me?"

I nodded.

"She picked me up, and between here and the Sidewalk Café I made some remark about how Tony and his dad didn't always get along. I shouldn't have said anything, but they'd been snarling at each other the night before, and I had it on my mind. Anyway, she brought it up for general lunchtime conversation."

"I remember. You cut her off very well."

"Lee, you know all about the situation between Mike and Tony. Tony just doesn't want to work in a restaurant, and Mike doesn't understand his attitude! But I didn't really want to go into it with Carolyn. I don't know yet how I managed to mention it to Julie."

Lindy was looking tired, so I did the dishes while she took the medicine the doctor had given her for headaches. She promised to lie down as soon as she locked the door after me. I headed back to the shop, but after I'd parked on Peach Street I walked across to Mercy Woodyard's insurance office, instead of going directly to my desk. I wanted to check on the bronze roses I'd ordered for her birthday.

I expected Joe's mother to mention the roses as soon as I walked in the door. After all, I'd signed the card "Joe and Lee."

But she didn't say a word. She accepted my birthday greetings in a friendly way, but she didn't mention the roses. And they weren't in sight in the office. When Mercy got a phone call, I even peeked into the inner office to see if she'd put them there, but there was no sign of any cut flowers.

We discussed the plans for her birthday celebrations—Mike Herrera was taking her out to dinner that evening, and Joe and I were taking both of them out the next week.

"I'll gain one year and ten pounds," Mercy said, smiling. "I don't deserve all this attention."

I went back to TenHuis Chocolade puzzled. Carolyn had promised to have the roses to Mercy before noon. Carolyn had an excellent professional reputation. If there was a problem with the flowers we'd ordered, I'd have expected her to call and explain.

Maybe, I thought, she'd called Joe. I'd better check with him.

I went into the shop and took my usual six deep breaths of chocolate aroma. I waved to Aunt Nettie, took off my coat, and reached for the telephone. Before I could punch in Joe's number, the door swung open, and Diane Denham rushed in.

She came straight into my office. "What's this I hear about someone attacking Lindy?"

"It happened last night. I just had lunch with her. She doesn't seem to be hurt badly."

"Oh, my goodness! First Julie, then these computer disasters, and now this! I can't believe it."

"How'd you hear about Lindy?"

"From Chief Jones! He was out at the inn. He wanted to know all about the Seventh Major Food Group. Are we the object of a vendetta?"

"That doesn't seem likely, Diane. We don't have all that much in common."

"Really we have nothing in common but that snoopy Julie."

"Snoopy? You found Julie snoopy?"

"Didn't you? She was always asking personal questions."

"I guess she was. The main thing I noticed about her questions was that she wouldn't answer them."

"She sure *asked* them. She should have been a detective."

"What do you mean, Diane?"

There was a moment of silence. Diane touched her beautiful white hair before she spoke. "Oh, never mind! I guess all of us have things we'd rather not talk about. Somehow Julie wormed them out of you."

"Wormed them out?"

"You sound just like her! She just kept asking until you discovered you'd told her things you didn't mean to." Diane gave an exasperated snort. "I only came by because I wanted to find out if Lindy had been hurt. Tell her I asked about her, okay? Oh, and I need four dozen crème de menthe bonbons. We've got a business conference coming in next weekend."

I left Diane roaming the office and shop while I went back to get her a box of crème de menthe bonbons. Lots of the Warner Pier B&Bs put these on the guests' pillows at turn-down time.

Diane paid for her bonbons and left without saying anything more about Julie. I was really puzzled. What had Diane been talking about? What had Julie known that Diane hadn't wanted known?

I remembered that I'd been planning to call Joe to see if he knew why his mother's flowers hadn't been delivered. I shook my head, picked up the phone and called the boat shop.

I'd almost decided Joe wasn't there when he picked up the phone. "Vintage Boats."

"Hi. It's Lee. You haven't heard from Carolyn Rose, have you?"

"Nope. Should I have?"

I told him that his mother's flowers apparently hadn't been delivered. "I was going to call Carolyn and ask about it, but I thought I'd better check with you. I didn't want to nag if she'd called to tell you there was some problem."

"I'll call her. After all, I'm paying the bill."

I left it to him and went back to work. In a few minutes, however, Joe called back. "I got the answering machine," he said. "I left a message."

"I could try her home."

Joe thought my offer over. "I hate to call business people at home, but—you know her pretty well. If you wouldn't mind . . ."

But the only answer I got at Carolyn's home was electronic—another answering machine. My stomach began to knot up. I wasn't annoyed. After all, Carolyn didn't have to answer to me. Was I worried? That wasn't quite the right description, either. I finally settled on concerned. So many strange things had been happening to members of the Seventh Major Food Group, having one of them out of touch made me concerned.

I tried to put Mercy's roses and Carolyn's whereabouts out of my mind. I organized my work. I had plenty of that. There was my own regular work, plus, that close to Valentine's Day I had to wait on the counter, since we wouldn't have any sales help until Tracy got out of school. Between the constant interruptions from walk-in customers and my concern—yes, that was definitely the right word—about Carolyn, I found it impossible to concentrate on the chocolate business.

When Tracy arrived, I simply gave up. I was so up in the air about Carolyn that I decided to drive out to her shop, then maybe to her home. At least I could see if the House of Roses van was in sight at either location.

It was around the side of her cute painted-lady shop.

My first reaction to seeing it was relief. Carolyn must have come in. I got out of my van, picked my way through the slush in her parking lot, crossed the wide Victorian veranda, and confidently reached for the door handle. It wouldn't budge. The door to the shop was locked.

I peered through the windows that flanked the center front door, mentally cursing their lace curtains and the elaborate arrangements of dolls and doilies, flowers and froufrou that Carolyn had dressed them with. I couldn't see inside.

I walked around to the side of the building. The side door had a glass window that looked into the office. At least it didn't have a lace curtain. But when I looked inside, nothing out of the ordinary was visible.

This was not reassuring. With the van there, Carlyn should be there, too. Her winter hours were roughly ten a.m. to four p.m. It was now three fifteen. She should be there. At least she should have taken care of Mercy's bronze roses. Or called either Joe or me to explain why she hadn't done so.

I walked on around the house. There was the window over the work sink, the one Jack Ingersoll had suspected had allowed a burglar to get into the shop. Thanks to my extreme height, I was able to peek into that. All I saw was an empty workroom. Empty of people, that is. A large box was on the stainless steel work table, and a tall glass vase stood beside it.

I went back to the van, climbed in, and called Carolyn's house on my cell phone. I talked to the answering machine again. Then I gnawed my nails.

But why was I so concerned? Because the shop ought to be open, and it wasn't? There was a ready explanation for that. Carolyn owned her own business. She could close up anytime she wanted to.

Was I concerned because the House of Roses van was there, and I knew it was Carolyn's only vehicle? There was a ready explanation for that, too. A friend could have come by to pick her up. They could be having a long lunch, visiting a museum, seeing a movie. Heck, Carolyn was a consenting adult. She could have gone off with a boyfriend and checked into a motel.

I just about convinced myself I was being silly. Then I thought about Mercy's roses, and I remembered something.

That box on the workroom table. It had printing on the side. And that tall glass vase beside it. It was exactly the kind of vase Carolyn and I had discussed using for Mercy's roses.

I jumped out of the van and plowed through the snow, back to the window that overlooked the workshop. Yes, my memory had been right. That box said "Grand Rapids Wholesale Flowers" on the side.

I was convinced that Carolyn had started to ar
range Mercy's flowers, but something had inter
rupted her. She had left without even putting th
flowers in her walk-in cooler. This was no casua
lunch date. Something was wrong.

I started to call 9-1-1, but I chickened out. I wa
simply afraid to talk to Hogan Jones, to tell him
was being nosy again.

So I called Joe, told him the whole story, and aske
him to call Hogan. After all, Hogan couldn't refus
a call from a fellow city official.

And he didn't. He agreed to come right out.

Joe came, too. He and I waited in the van whil
one of the patrolmen, Jerry Cherry, jimmied the bac
window and climbed inside.

Carolyn's body was under the work table.

Chapter 11

Carolyn was dead, but it was hours before I knew anything more than that.

As the investigators began to gather, and it became obvious that they didn't need me hanging around, I drove back to the shop. The chief told Joe to follow me. I had the feeling Hogan wanted him with me, not because he was worried about my emotional needs, but because he was concerned for my physical safety.

I made it to the shop safely. By then it was close to five o'clock and everyone was leaving. Aunt Nettie, Joe, and I huddled in the break room. Then I thought about Lindy—who'd barely escaped an attack the evening before—and I called her. She was fine, she said. The kids were home from school, her mother was there playing Monopoly with them, and a Warner Pier patrolman had just pulled into the drive.

That was reassuring, but I was still worried about the rest of the Seventh Major Food Group. Whether they were friends or suspects, I wanted to know if they were all right. I went to the office and called each of them. Jason didn't answer, but I left a message on his machine. Margaret answered on the first ring. Like Lindy, she also had a house full of kids, and she said a Holland policeman had been by to check all her doors and windows. Her husband was on the way home. Diane and Ronnie Denham also said they were all right, but Diane was too upset to tell me any more than that.

I was just breathing a sigh of relief when someone banged loudly on the door. I whirled to look. It was dark outside, but when I went close to the window in the shop's front door, I could see a face. It was Martin Schrader.

He didn't seem to be armed, and Joe and Aunt Nettie were there, so I let him in. At the moment Martin didn't look at all like the suave businessman I'd seen at Julie's memorial service. His distinguished gray hair was hidden by a warm hat, and instead of a tailor-made suit, he wore a navy blue down jacket. But the change in him was more than his wardrobe. His face didn't look suave either. It looked pinched and worried.

When he spoke, his voice was shrill. "What's happened out at House of Roses?"

I looked at Joe, wondering if I should talk about it. Joe shrugged. "It'll be all over town by now," he said.

I told Martin that Carolyn was dead. "We don't know any details," I said. "I got worried about her, and—with Joe to back me up—I more or less demanded that the shop be checked out. But the chief sent us home after they found her body."

Suddenly I remembered that Martin Schrader didn't know either Joe or Aunt Nettie, so I introduced them.

He acknowledged the introductions with an absent-minded nod. "I can't believe this," he said. "Carolyn! Of all people. She was the original take-charge woman. The last person I'd expect to be the victim of a crime."

"Why?" I said.

My question seemed to surprise Martin. His eyes widened, then narrowed, and he walked up and down the shop a few steps. "I'm not sure why I said that. I guess I had the feeling that if someone tried to attack Carolyn, she'd tear them limb from limb."

"Carolyn did tend to be outspoken," I said, "but I wouldn't have expected her to have a lot of physical prowler. I mean, prowess! I don't think she was particularly strong."

"Her tongue could skin a man alive," Martin said.

"I'm glad to say she never spoke that harshly to me. But I can see her being aggressive."

"Aggressive! That's not a strong enough word." He stopped talking and looked at each of us. "I assume all of you know I dated Carolyn for a while—actually, several years back."

I nodded, and I guess Joe and Aunt Nettie did, too. "Warner Pier is a small town," Joe said.

"Yes. Well, one time my mother was down for the weekend, and she needed a prescription refilled. Carolyn and I went over to the Superette to pick it up. We took the bottle along, because naturally the pharmacist had to call her doctor in Grand Rapids and get an okay. And that druggist—the one who talks so much—"

"Greg Glossop." Joe, Aunt Nettie, and I spoke in unison.

"Anyway, he gave us the wrong medication. And Carolyn noticed right away."

"Good for her," Aunt Nettie said.

"Yes, that was fine. But what wasn't fine was the way Carolyn tore into him about it. I simply couldn't believe the way she talked to him. Then Carolyn acted—well, as if I ought to be *pleased* at the way she'd behaved." Martin frowned. "Believe me, if

Mother had heard her—*she* definitely wouldn't have been pleased. After that I was always nervous about bringing Carolyn around Mother. Eventually we quit seeing each other."

And you felt that you'd had a narrow escape, I thought.

Joe and I exchanged quick glances, and I thought Joe's lips almost twitched into a grin before he spoke. "I'd heard Carolyn had a sharp temper. But I barely knew her. How well did she know Julie?"

"Julie!" Martin pulled his dark cap off with an exasperated gesture. "I don't know how Julie got mixed up with her. I nearly fell over when Carolyn showed up at the memorial service."

"Julie sought her out," I said. "Julie said she wanted all the party planning business from around Warner Pier. She was quite up front about wanting to make professional contacts down here. And Carolyn would have been a good contact for her. She had quite a successful business during the summer season, decorated for a lot of the big parties the summer people give. She and Julie could have referred business to each other. But I never got a hint that Julie knew that you and Carolyn had dated each other."

Martin shook his head. "Julie and Carolyn were exact opposites. Picturing them exchanging friendly e-mails boggles the mind."

"It's even stranger that they seem to have shared the same fate," Joe said.

Martin shuddered. "Murdered by intruders in their own spaces."

Joe spoke again. "How did you find out something had happened to Carolyn?"

"I drove by there and saw all the police cars."

"Okay, but why did you come here? I mean, to TenHuis Chocolade. How did you know Lee was involved?"

"As I drove by House of Roses, I saw Ms. McKinney pulling out of the parking lot. I guess you were behind her, in that pickup that's outside. When I saw all the law enforcement and an ambulance, I knew something bad had happened at Carolyn's shop."

Martin gave a guilty smile. "I guess I needed some Dutch courage. I went down to the Sidewalk Café and had a scotch—getting my nerve up to come and ask Ms. McKinney—Lee—what happened. I hadn't had the courage to pull in at Carolyn's, the way I had planned."

I felt surprised. "I thought you weren't seeing her anymore."

"I hadn't seen Carolyn for several years."

"Then why were you planning to go by the shop?"

Martin ran a hand through his hair. "Oh, didn't I tell you? Carolyn called my office yesterday. Left a message with my assistant. She asked me to come to see her. She said she had some information she thought I'd want."

I thought about that one for a minute. It was a surprise. Carolyn had discussed Martin with me the previous day, but she hadn't sounded as if she planned to be in contact with him.

What on earth could have inspired her call?

While I was thinking, Joe was doing his attorney act, quizzing Martin. All that Carolyn had told the assistant, Martin said, was that she had some information he might want. He'd had no idea what Carolyn's information had been. He'd been staying down at the Warner Pier house, but he'd gotten the message when he made a routine call to his office.

"You need to tell Chief Jones about that call," Joe said.

"Sure, if he has time to talk to me. There's no secret about the call, but I have no idea what Carolyn wanted to tell me, and I doubt it had anything to do with her death." Then Martin looked at his watch. "I'll call the chief in the morning. I told Brad I'd take him to dinner. We need to talk about Julie's estate."

"At one point you wanted to talk to me," I said. "Has that situation resolved itself?"

"Not really." Martin pulled a pocket date book out from inside his winter jacket and consulted it. "How about lunch tomorrow?" He turned toward Joe, including him in the invitation. "Sidewalk Café?"

Joe declined, but I accepted for one o'clock. Martin wrote the date in his book, then zipped his jacket. "I guess I'd better head back to the house to meet Brad."

"Are you and Brad both staying there?" Joe asked.

"Brad actually lives on the property and drives to Grand Rapids every day. I'm just down for a business meeting early tomorrow."

A business meeting? What business could Martin Schrader have that couldn't be done better in Grand Rapids? I almost asked, but decided that would be entirely too nosy, even for me. So Martin put his warm hat back on, and I unlocked and opened the shop's street door for him.

"I know Carolyn's death is a real shock to you," I said, "coming on top of losing Julie."

He looked at me with eyes that were as black as Julie's had been. And suddenly they looked really miserable. "Carolyn and I—well, I almost married her. Even though we had grown apart, yes, it's still a shock."

Married? The word jogged my memory. "Oh!" I yelped out the sound, then grabbed Martin's sleeve and tugged him back inside the shop. "I'd been wanting to ask you something!"

Martin looked wary, but he came back inside.

"Who was Julie married to?" I said.

He scowled. I had the feeling he didn't want to answer.

"I know I'm simply being nosy," I said. "But

Julie—well, she had a way of getting people to tell her things. But she never told the rest of us anything about herself. Nobody on the Seventh Major Food Group newslist had any idea she'd been married."

"The marriage was over. It doesn't really matter who Julie married. He was just a whiner."

I persisted. "For one thing, Julie seemed so young. She didn't seem old enough to have been married."

"Julie was twenty-eight."

"Twenty-eight! She looked about twenty-one. Of course, I knew she went to high school with Margaret Van Meter, but I put Margaret at about twenty-five—in spite of all those kids."

Martin looked confused. "All those kids? Now who is this?"

"Never mind," I said. "I'm dithering. I'm just surprised. I'm surprised to learn Julie was as old as she was, and I was surprised to learn she'd been married and hadn't ever mentioned it."

"Nobody around Grand Rapids and Holland knew," Martin said. "Julie didn't want an official announcement made, so it never got in the paper. Their wedding was very small. They didn't even tell Mother until it was over. Then Julie said she didn't want a bunch of presents. Said it would make her new husband uncomfortable."

I'd learned a few things from watching Joe-the-lawyer ask questions. I kept quiet. Just looked expectant.

It worked, I guess. After a few seconds Martin went on. "Julie had gone back east to college. She got a degree in French, then started on her masters in art history. This fellow was a graduate assistant in the English Department." He gave an exasperated snort. "Like I say, he was a real whiner. Julie said he wouldn't come out to Michigan to meet the family, so Mother went to Boston to meet him. She wasn't impressed. She said he was an 'I'm gonna go eat worms' type. He seemed to be embarrassed because Julie's family had money. But it didn't keep him from marrying her!"

I nodded encouragingly, and Martin kept talking. "I had to take a trip to New York, so I went up to meet him. Julie's parents were dead. It seemed as if somebody should show an interest. I got the same impression Mother did. Julie had dropped out of graduate school, told her grandmother she couldn't accept an allowance any longer. She was working for a big country club, planning their special events. That didn't please her husband. It wasn't intellectual enough for him. But he didn't mind her paying the rent so he could play the part of misunderstood genius!"

"I can see how Julie might have gotten mixed up with a guy like that," I said. "She was always sympathetic to everyone."

"Yes! And when the whiner finally had some success," Martin said, "he walked out on her! If uncles were still allowed to go after young whippersnappers who did their nieces wrong—believe me, I'd have been there with my horsewhip!"

He turned back to the door. "So Julie never mentioned him to anyone, huh? I'm glad she had that much pride."

"I guess the police looked at him, made sure he wasn't around the night she was killed?"

"Oh, the creep had no motive for killing her. Besides, he was at a big dinner in New York that night. Now that he's famous."

"He's famous?"

"In some circles." Martin opened the door. Then he used his final comment as an exit line.

"Julie's ex-husband is Seth Blackman. He won some big literary prize last year. He was speaking to the assembled intelligentsia of New York City the night Julie was killed."

Chapter 12

The minute the door was locked behind Martin I headed for my office. Joe was already there, leaning over to hit the button that turned the computer on.

He moved to let me sit in my chair. "Let's Google him," he said.

"It's nice to know you're as nosy as I am," I said.

Joe laughed, and Aunt Nettie, who never touches the computer, said plaintively, "What are you two up to?"

Joe explained how to use the search engine Google while I called up the screen and typed in "Seth Blackman."

"I hope I'm spelling it right," I said.

"If nothing likely comes up, we'll try Blackman with an 'o,' " Joe said. "Or 'ond.' "

But Blackman with an "a" seemed to be correct. We got a whole screenful of results. In the next twenty minutes we learned that Seth Blackman had been a graduate student at an elite New England college. His first novel had been published eighteen months ago, and the previous spring that novel had been named winner of the Bookman Prize. Whatever that was.

I might not know anything about the Bookman Prize, but winning it was earning Seth Blackman's novel a lot of attention. We found references to articles on him in the *New York Review of Books*, the *Atlantic Monthly*, and a number of other magazines a mere Michigan accountant had never heard of. Joe said he hadn't heard of most of them, either. "Literary," he said. "Which means circulation limited to English majors."

"Wait a minute," I said. "Here's a review with a description of the plot."

Joe leaned over my shoulder, and we read it together. "In this dark comedy, Adam Greening, a brilliant young writer, finds himself stifled artistically," the article said. "Pitied by his beautiful and wealthy, but immature, wife—whose maudlin and oversentimental mind cannot grasp his artistic ambitions—he struggles to achieve the worldly success she would be able to understand. His scholarly achievements fail to impress her or her family of Philistines, who condescendingly offer financial help. Finally, her shallow outlook on life leads him to take his own life."

I read it out loud, and Aunt Nettie looked puzzled. "How can the review call it a 'comedy,' if it ends in the main character's suicide?"

"It says it's a 'dark comedy,' " I said. "It goes on to say the wife is 'a hilarious picture of middle-class anti-intellectualism.' "

"Reading between the lines," Joe said, "I'd guess that Martin Schrader was exactly right about Seth Blackman. The guy is a whiner."

"It doesn't sound like a very good book," Aunt Nettie said. "But how does it reflect on Julie's ex-husband's character?"

Joe pointed to the screen. "I never met Julie, but

the description of the book sounds as if he skewered her. He wrote a semiautobiographical novel—he gave us a broad hint about that, because his name is Seth Blackman and his hero's name is Adam Greening. Then he used the situation in which he found himself—a poor graduate student married to a girl who came from a wealthy family—as a plot device. This would appear to be deliberately designed to make the reader assume that Blackman used Julie as the model of the main character's wife, a 'maudlin and oversentimental' woman. Which, by the way, is a repetitious and redundant description by this high-falutin reviewer."

"He made fun of his own wife? But that's mean!" Aunt Nettie said.

"I agree," I said. "Martin Schrader was definitely right. The guy should be horsewhipped. On the other hand, I'm embarrassed. Apparently the things Julie's ex made fun of her about are exactly the things I found annoying. The overly sentimental poems and silly jokes. The gushing way of speaking."

"But, Lee," Joe said, "if you complained, you just did it to friends."

"I don't think I ever mentioned it to anybody but Aunt Nettie and Lindy. When I asked Julie to cut it out, I tried to be tactful."

"Right. You didn't publish a novel making fun of her. Besides, judging by what Martin said, Seth Blackman wrote the novel while she was supporting him, earning a good proportion of the living for the two of them. And she gave up her own graduate work to do it. Seth Blackman's assessment of Julie may have had some justice. She may well have been overly sentimental. But that's not the point. You don't hold people you care about—or once cared about—up for public ridicule."

Yeah, the way Joe had never made any public statement about the breakup of his marriage to Clementine Ripley, no matter how many tabloid reporters asked him about it. For a minute I remembered how much I appreciated him.

But I didn't say anything about that when I spoke again. "It sure explains why Julie never mentioned that she'd been married. This must have been a humiliating experience."

"It also explains why Martin didn't want anybody to know Julie had been mixed up with Seth Blackman. Judging from this plot synopsis, I'd guess that Blackman let the whole Schrader family have it. Embarrassed all of them."

Aunt Nettie shook her head. "It doesn't sound as if Julie and her ex-husband were very well-suited."

"To say the least," I said. "But this Internet stuff does make one thing certain. Unless he hired a hit man, Seth Blackman is not a suspect in Julie's death. As Martin said, he was giving a speech at a literary dinner in New York that night. The *New York Times* even had quotes. And a photo."

We all took a look at Julie's ex-husband. He was one of these soulful types—hair a little too long, eyes a little too sensitive.

"Too bad he was at that dinner," Aunt Nettie said. "It sounds as if he deserves to go to prison, just for general meanness, and now he won't. But I guess I'll go home. Do you two need to stay here until you talk to Hogan?"

"Probably not," I said. "He'll know where to find us."

Joe offered to bring a pizza out to the house, and Aunt Nettie said she had ingredients for a salad in the refrigerator. I followed her home, and Joe came a half hour later, bearing a large pepperoni with mushrooms. I hadn't expected to be hungry, but I discovered that I was.

Joe and I had just split the last slice of pizza when the phone rang. I jumped up. "Maybe that's Hogan."

But it wasn't Hogan's basso on the phone. It was a timid little voice. "Lee? It's Margaret. You weren't in bed, were you?"

I looked at my watch. "It's only eight thirty, Margaret. I don't usually go to bed this early. What are you up to?"

"I finally got all the kids settled, and I wanted to know more about Carolyn. I didn't like to ask when you called. I'm trying not to talk about all this in front of them."

"If you want details, Margaret—"

"Oh, no!"

"Good, because I don't have any."

"But do the police think that Carolyn's death had something to do with Julie's?"

"They haven't told me that, but it's hard not to see a connection."

"I hardly knew Carolyn. Was she anything like Julie?"

"I talked to Martin Schrader today, and he said she was the complete opposite of Julie in every way. I think that's right. Carolyn could talk really rough; Julie was sweet and gushy. Julie was always doing people favors; Carolyn was more competitive. Carolyn was cynical; Julie was sentimental."

Margaret's voice took on a sarcastic tone. "Oh, yes. Julie was sentimental."

It was the first comment I'd ever heard from Margaret that sounded critical of anybody. I was surprised it would be Julie.

"I found her a little too sentimental," I said. "But she had lots of good qualities. I guess you'd known her a lot longer than I had."

"Since high school. I'm ready to forget high school, if you want to know the truth. And Julie was trying to drag me into plans for our tenth reunion."

"Oh, gee! I guess somebody has to do it."

"Maybe so. But it doesn't have to be me. I've *atoned*

for what happened in high school. I didn't want my nose rubbed in it. It's time to move on."

Margaret muttered a good-bye and hung up, leaving me with my mouth agape. Margaret had "atoned" for high school? What did that mean?

I thought over my own high school years. I'd done a lot of stupid things, things I regretted, and since graduation I'd learned to deal with the memory of being a dumb teenager. But I didn't think I'd use the word "atoned" when I talked about the process of growing up. The word had a sad sound. What had happened to make Margaret feel that she had to "atone" for her high school behavior? Most of us laughed at the silly things we'd done.

At least Margaret was all right. Nobody had broken into her house or shot out her windows or anything else dire. She was safe for the moment, as Lindy and the Denhams seemed to be.

But what about Jason? I'd never gotten hold of him. I looked up his home phone and called. It was a relief to hear his voice.

Jason had, of course, already heard about Carolyn. "Yeah," he said. "I thought I was getting arrested. I was down at the hardware store, and the cops drew up with sirens blaring."

"Why'd they do that?"

"Chief Jones said all the Seventh Food Group members might be in danger. They called the restaurant, and Ross told them where I'd gone. I wish they hadn't been so dramatic about it. I was perfectly all right."

"And how's your computer?"

"All reloaded and working. All I lost permanently was my e-mail." Jason gave another exasperated sigh. "I'm awfully sorry about Carolyn, but I didn't know her well. I'm shocked, but not saddened, if you know what I mean."

"I guess I feel the same way. She was prickly and

hard to get to know. Not like Julie, who was maddening, but more loveable."

There was a moment of silence before Jason replied. "Right," he said. "Julie could be maddening, but she was basically a nice person."

His guarded answer had roused my curiosity. I decided to follow up. "Jason, you introduced the rest of us to Julie. How did you meet her?"

"Working a party last summer. I was tending bar—one of my moonlighting jobs—at a party in Holland. Some bigwig had taken over one of those restaurants right on the yacht harbor for a wedding reception. I guess Julie knew the couple. Anyway, she was running the show—over the objections of the restaurant catering staff. I'd been hired by the restaurant, but I didn't like the catering manager." Jason laughed. "I backed Julie, did some rearranging to get things the way she wanted them. The catering manager walked out in a huff, and Julie and I wound up in charge. I haven't been asked to tend bar there again."

"I can't imagine why not."

"I wouldn't go if they asked, unless they get a new catering manager. But after that Julie gave me a ring a couple of times, asked me to help with parties. I liked her ideas, and she wasn't hard to work with. With the new restaurant opening, we could have done some nice events. I can work with anybody—except that one catering manager."

I laughed. "I did notice a few qualifications in your opinion of Julie, however."

Jason's voice became wary. "Oh? What did I say?"

" 'Thoughtless' was one of the words used in some e-mail. And you didn't have any trouble agreeing to 'maddening.' "

"Nobody's perfect. You let her have it, too. Over those jokes and poems."

"Yeah, but that wasn't 'thoughtless,' Jason. Julie

was almost too sweet and kind around me. What did she pull to change your opinion of her?"

Jason didn't answer, so I spoke in a moment. "Sorry. That was a nosy question."

"Oh, it's all right. All our friends know. She caused Ross some problems."

Ross. Jason's partner. "Oh," I said. "I've never met Ross."

"He's a good guy. We've been together for five years, you know, but Ross was married for fifteen. He has grown kids. Ross's dad is an old military type, a retired sergeant. He's in a nursing home in Holland, barely creeps around with a walker. He's never confronted Ross's lifestyle—and there's no reason he has to. When Ross and I moved in together, Ross's dad just acted as if we were saving money. Oh, I'm sure he realized the situation wasn't just platonic, but nothing has ever been said.

"Then Julie showed up, one day when we were out at the nursing home. She needed to give me something, and it was a handy place to meet. She was damn sweet and gracious to Ross's dad. I was appreciating her nice attitude, when she makes some remark about her ambition to plan 'a lovely wedding for Ross and Jason.' "

"Oh, no!"

"Ross's dad—the poor old guy got tears in his eyes. He and Ross have had their problems over the years, but things are at least on an even keel between them now, and we don't want to have any kind of confrontation—with the sergeant's health being so bad. When I objected, she lectured me about confronting my problems, about being honest."

"That was rude!"

Jason took a deep breath. "I know this isn't a smart thing to say, considering recent events, but right at that moment I could have killed Julie. But I got over it."

Jason and I said a few more words, and I hung up. That Julie. Thoughtless. Yes, Jason had used the right word for her. And I thought I was nosy; I wasn't in the running compared to her. I went back to Joe and Aunt Nettie shaking my head.

I wondered what Martin Schrader would have to say about Julie when I met him for lunch the next day.

CHOCOLATE CHAT

HUMOROUS CHOCOLATE

"Strength is the capacity to break a chocolate bar into four pieces with your bare hands—and then eat just one of the pieces."   —Judith Viorst

"Research tells us fourteen out of any ten individuals like chocolate."   —Sandra Boynton

"There are two kinds of people in the world. Those who love chocolate and communists."
    —Leslie Moak Murray in *Murray's Law* comic strip

"All I really need is love, but a little chocolate now and then doesn't hurt!"   —Lucy Van Pelt

"The 12-step chocoholic program: NEVER BE MORE THAN 12 STEPS AWAY FROM CHOCOLATE!"
                    —Terry Moore

"My therapist told me the way to achieve true inner peace is to finish what I start. So far today, I have finished two bags of M&M's and a chocolate cake. I feel better already."   —Dave Barry

Chapter 13

Joe and I made our official statements on Carolyn's death the next morning. I think Hogan had been meeting with the Holland detectives until late the previous night. I know law enforcement had been busy.

Other than that, the morning was routine—or as routine as a chocolate business can be three weeks before Valentine's Day. I had nothing more to cope with than a dozen last-minute orders for multiple fancy holiday pieces—delivery ASAP—and walk-in customers. Dolly Jolly took care of a lot of the counter business for me. I could hear her voice boom. "A quarter-pound box of raspberry cream bonbons! And a half-pound of assorted truffles and bonbons! One minute!"

Only one e-mail showed up that was unrelated to the holiday, but that one seemed significant. The Seventh Major Food Group was revived.

A message came from Jason. "I had a call from Vince Veldkamp," Jason wrote. "He's run Veldkamp Used Food Equipment and Supply forever, but now he says he's selling out and retiring. All his inventory is going on the block. If anybody's interested, he says we can have a sneak preview Friday night at the Holland store. Lee, he says he's got a cooling tunnel and some other stuff left over from the closeout of Vanderkool's Chocolate. And Lindy, is Mike still looking for a freezer for Herrera's? Vince has one that sounds good.''

I checked with Aunt Nettie and e-mailed back that we would definitely be interested in the cooling tunnel if the price was right. Aunt Nettie would also be interested in work tables and storage racks.

I found Jason's message comforting. It seemed to be a symbol that—someday—life would return to normal. The Seventh Food Group would go back to discussing professional concerns, instead of worrying about all of us getting killed. It made Dolly's calls to customers seem comforting as well. I reminded myself that TenHuis Chocolade was having a good Valentine season. Aunt Nettie and I had worked hard to get the business back on a firm financial footing, and it was comforting to know we'd made it, at least for the moment.

I needed that comfort when I thought about my planned lunch with Martin Schrader. I wasn't looking forward to it. I hadn't dressed in my black pants suit with the severe silk shirt and the heavy boots—I'd settled for brown flannel slacks and a sage green turtleneck—but I'd felt like wearing an intimidating outfit. Big business types like Uncle Martin can over-awe me, and I didn't want to be trampled underfoot. I didn't understand why Martin wanted to talk to me; I only knew it was likely to be touchy, since it would concern his murdered niece.

The day was crisp and sunny, so at one o'clock the half-block walk down to the Sidewalk Café gave me a nice breath of fresh air. The Sidewalk Café's decor is a pun. Although it does have an outdoor dining area—closed in January, of course—that's not the reason for the restaurant's name. The café is designed to look like a sidewalk. Sidewalk toys—roller skates, tricycles, jump ropes, scooters—are hung on the walls. The floor is cement and is painted with designs that copy childish graffiti and hopscotch layouts. The restaurant is lighthearted, and the sandwiches, soups, and salads on the lunch menu are good.

When I came in, Mike Herrera greeted me. In his combined roles as my best friend's father-in-law, my boyfriend's mother's boyfriend, my boyfriend's boss, and the mayor of the town I live in, Mike has plenty of personal impact on my life. He's also the only other native of Texas I've identified as living in Warner Pier. He grew up in Denton, just north of Dallas.

Mike made himself a successful businessman the old-fashioned way; he worked day and night for years, and he's still not too good to bus tables or fry bacon if that's what needs doing in one of his three restaurants. He's an attractive man—a sort of heavy-set Latin lover.

"Hi, Lee," Mike said. "You getting a sandwich to go or can I entice you into a real lunch?"

"I'm meeting Martin Schrader for lunch, Mike. Has he come in yet?"

Mike waggled an eyebrow to show he was about to make a joke. "Does Joe know about this?"

"Joe was invited along, but declined. Martin wants to talk to me about his niece."

"I'll give you the quiet corner." Mike grabbed a couple of menus and led me toward the back of the restaurant. "I want to talk to Martin Schrader myself, but maybe this isn't a good time."

"What do you want to talk to him about?"

"His mother's property. It's so close to Warner Pier that the city planning commission has begun to wonder what's going to happen to it after Mrs. Schrader passes on."

"You're on your own with that topic, Mike. I couldn't possibly bring it up."

"I can do my own political dirty work. How about a drink? Mimosa?"

"Have you got any real Texas iced tea?"

"I'll make you some."

There are wonderful cooks and restaurants in Michigan, but rarely do they understand iced tea. For one thing, they think it's only a hot weather drink. We Texans see it as standard fare year-round.

There are other differences. Iced tea cannot be made from mix as it almost always is in Michigan restaurants; it must be brewed from real tea. And it can't be served over a couple of anemic ice cubes. It has to be poured over a whole glass of ice cubes or cracked ice. The sugar and lemon are optional—at least in my part of Texas. This differs from the deep South. There, I understand, people want "sweet tea," which requires that the hot tea be poured over sugar, so that it dissolves thoroughly. Sweet tea is a fine drink, but I'm satisfied with the unsweetened version. If there is a lemon, however, it should be cut into a wedge, not a disk.

There are a lot of nuances to iced tea. Sometimes I think Mike and I are the only two people in Warner Pier who understand the drink.

Mike had just served me a tall, refreshing glass when I looked through the big front window of the Sidewalk Café and saw Martin Schrader get out of a large dark sedan. He stood bent over, looking back into the car for a few seconds, obviously saying good-bye. Then he slammed the door, and I caught a glimpse of a logo—black and white with a red wing-shaped thing sticking up—but I couldn't read the writing underneath. Martin swung around and came into the restaurant, unzipping his down jacket. He paused near the door, obviously trying to adjust his eyes to the change in light level, and Mike appeared from the kitchen and led him back to the corner table.

"I'm sorry to keep you waiting," Martin said. "My meeting ran a little longer than I expected."

"That's quite all right. It gave Mike time to make me some Texas tea."

Martin looked puzzled. "I thought Texas tea was slang for oil."

"It may be. But to Texans like Mike and me, it merely means well-brewed, properly iced tea."

Martin promptly proved himself a real Michiganian. He shivered. "Too cold for iced tea," he said. "Though I could use a Bloody Mary."

I refrained from remarking that a Bloody Mary was just as cold as a glass of iced tea. Martin ordered one; then he and I chitchatted idly while we selected and ordered our lunches. I went with the vegetable soup and cheese biscuits special, and Martin ordered a bleu cheese burger with a side of fries.

Then silence fell, and so did my stomach. We'd put off talking about Julie as long as possible.

We both spoke at once.

"About Julie—" I said.

"Thanks for agreeing to talk to me—" Martin said.

Then, of course, we had to stop and do the politeness thing—"You first." "No, you first."—before I prompted Martin. "You said you want to talk about Julie. Unfortunately, I don't really know a lot about her. As I told you, I didn't even know she'd been married."

"How did you find that out?"

"Oh, Brad mentioned it."

Martin's eyes opened wide. "Brad? At the funeral?"

Whoops. I'd forgotten Brad had asked me not to tell Martin that he'd been by my office. "Oh, I ran into Brad one day in Warner Pier."

I raced on, trying to change the subject. "Anyway, Brad didn't say much about Julie's marriage. But after you gave me his name, I looked Seth Blackman up on the Internet, and it sounds as if he's a real jerk. I can understand Julie not wanting to talk about him. But she didn't talk about anything else personal either—at least with the Seventh Major Food Group. Have you tried her other friends?"

Martin sipped his Bloody Mary before he answered. "That's one of the things that bothered me about Julie. She had practically become a recluse."

"She seemed to be getting some business."

"Yes, she made the rounds of restaurants and caterers. But she didn't get out socially. No dates. No movies with her friends."

"Did you try Margaret Van Meter? Apparently Julie used to go by and see her."

Martin pulled out his pocket calendar and wrote Margaret's name down, then promised to call her.

"I'm afraid I haven't been any help to you," I said. "What I know about Julie is not worth lunch."

"Oh, I haven't asked you the real question." He took another gulp of Bloody Mary. He was apparently having trouble asking that "real" question. I tried to put an expectant look on my face, and he finally spoke.

"Did Julie ever indicate that she was afraid of anything? Of anybody?"

I thought about it. Then I shook my head. "No, I don't recall her saying or doing anything that indicated she was afraid. Does that mean you're not buying the theory that Julie was killed by a burglar?"

"I'm not saying that idea is wrong. It just seems—well—dumb to assume that that's the case. I wouldn't want to see the police consider that as the only possibility."

"If they had that idea, it seems as if the killing of Carolyn would bring that theory into question."

Our food came then, and Martin didn't answer until he'd taken a bite of hamburger. "I talked to the

Holland detectives this morning. They're not sharing their ideas with me. But if I could have something specific to tell them, some incident, some remark Julie had made—well, it might point them in a different direction."

"Brad and Julie seemed to be in contact fairly often. I assume you've asked him."

Martin's eyes flickered toward me; then he dropped them and concentrated on his French fries. "Brad didn't have anything to say about it."

"We could look Julie's e-mails over," I said.

"You still have them?"

"Oh, yes. I'm notorious for not cleaning out my delete file for months at a time. I'm sure everything I've ever had from Julie is still in there. You're welcome to look at it."

"I'd appreciate that."

I laughed. "You didn't need to give me lunch to get a look at my delete file. I assure you there are no secrets in it. Just a bunch of chocolate orders and the occasional note from my mother. A phone call would have done the trick."

Martin responded gallantly, lifting his Bloody Mary glass. "But this is extremely pleasant. I'm enjoying getting acquainted."

I smiled. "I do have one nosy question I'd like to ask, however. Did you ever find Julie's mouse?"

"No! It's never turned up. How did you know about the mouse?"

I sketched my conversation with Hogan Jones, explaining that he was a close friend of my aunt's. "I'm afraid he and I thought it was funny. We kept picturing the Holland crime scene crew searching, afraid to lift an afghan or open a drawer for fear the mouse would pop out at them."

Martin smiled. "That could happen, but if it did they didn't tell me. I set a live trap, but as far as I know Blondie has never turned up."

"Blondie? The mouse's name is Blondie?"

"Right. As in ash blond. Julie was always partial to white mice. Now Brad, he likes the brown ones."

"Somehow brown ones don't seem as petlike. Too much like what we set traps for in my aunt's Michigan basement."

I guess it had become obvious that we weren't having a serious conversation, because Mike appeared, bearing a tray of dessert selections. "Pick one," he said. "On the house."

"Looks great," Martin said. "But I shouldn't eat too much. I've got to drive to Grand Rapids this afternoon. I don't want to fall asleep."

"I'll put it in a box, if you'd rather," Mike said. "Of course, I'm going to ask for some information in exchange."

Martin looked a little wary, but he nodded, and Mike pulled up a chair. "I'm putting on my Mayor of Warner Pier hat," he said. "I'm curious about the Schrader family property down here. Since it adjoins Warner Pier on the south and it's a big chunk of undeveloped land . . ."

Martin shook his head. "Mike, I can't tell you a thing."

"I noticed that, when your niece died, the family picked the Lake Michigan Conservation Society for memorial gifts."

"That was Brad's idea. My mother went along with it." Then Martin gave a deep sigh. "Look, there's a family trust, and Brad and I are both beneficiaries. But the Warner Pier property is not part of the trust. It belongs to my mother outright. She can do anything she wants to with it—and I assure you she will! If you want to see it go to the Conservation Society—"

"No! No! The city doesn't have a policy that covers it. We're simply curious. We have to think about what might happen." Mike leaned closer to Martin and lowered his voice. "To tell the truth, I'd like to see all these big family properties remain with the families. But very few families can keep them these days."

Martin nodded. "Taxes."

"Taxes." Mike grinned. "And, of course, with the property outside our city limits, Warner Pier isn't getting a cut."

"Mike," Martin said, "if I get a hint of my mother's plans, I'll tip you off."

"That's all I'm asking. A tip would definitely be worth a piece of cheesecake."

We all laughed. Martin selected a piece of turtle cheesecake as his freebie, and I asked for bread pudding. Mike promised to send us coffee, then left.

"You were very gracious to Mike," I said. "He was being extremely nosy."

Martin shrugged. "My grandfather bought that property in 1935 for practically nothing. It wasn't good for orchards, so nobody wanted it. Now it's going to be one of the biggest items in my mother's estate."

"How is your mother? I mean, the word around west Michigan is that her health isn't good."

"She has good days and bad days. She's nearly ninety. She has arthritis and a pacemaker."

"Julie looked a lot like her."

Martin's eyes widened. "Yes, she did. Or she looked a lot like Mother looked when she was Julie's age. But how did you know?"

"The eyes. Black and snapping. They both could look right through you."

Martin blinked. Had I made him cry?

"Sorry," I said. "It just struck me when I met Mrs. Schrader. Now, gobble up your cheesecake, and we'll go look at the e-mail."

We made light conversation while we drank our coffee. Martin paid the bill and said good-bye to

Mike. We both put on our hats and zipped up our jackets, then walked the half-block to TenHuis Chocolade. I led the way into the office and plopped into my chair.

"Hang your jacket on the coat tree, if you like," I said. "This will take only a minute." I didn't bother to go online, but went straight to "deleted items."

When the folder opened, it took me a few minutes to realize that it held only a couple of dozen items.

The only Seventh Food Group message in it was the one I'd received from Jason that morning. Everything I'd received before Wednesday, a day earlier, had disappeared.

Chapter 14

I did everything I could think of. I checked the computer's main recycle bin, looked in my other e-mail folders, wracked my brain, used shocking language, and pulled out handfuls of hair. But my deleted and sent e-mail folders were empty, and my recycle bin was, too.

Martin Schrader reacted as if it were his fault, apologizing at length.

"Don't be silly," I said, when I was able to say anything that wasn't a swear word. "It has nothing to do with you. You just happened to be on the spot when I found out that the folders were gone. Actually, I can't believe I'm so lucky."

"Lucky?"

"Yes. Other members of the Seventh Food Group have had computer trouble, and they lost everything." I explained that Carolyn, Jason, and the Denhams all had their business records wiped out.

"Then Lindy Herrera was physically attacked, and her laptop was stolen," I said. "I seem to be getting off easy. Besides, I backed up my business records after all the others had trouble, and I've updated the disk every day since then."

"So you have a copy of your e-mail?"

I shook my head. "I'm afraid not." I reached into my drawer and pulled out my backup disk. "I didn't see any reason to back up my e-mail. I get a lot of orders in by e-mail, true, but I print them out or move them to different folders as I read them. Ordinarily I don't put anything in the delete file except things I'm through with, like messages from my mother or Seventh Food Group chitchat. When I backed up my files, I only backed up correspondence, accounting—things like that."

Martin looked extremely troubled. "Have you talked to the police about these computer problems?"

Martin seemed to think he was the first person who had thought of that. I tried to be polite when I told him I'd already been over it with Chief Jones, and that Hogan had passed that idea on to the Holland detectives.

"Of course, it wouldn't hurt if you talked to them as well," I said. I guess I thought an important businessman like Martin Schrader might have more clout with the police than a group of small business owners like the Seventh Food Group.

Martin left, and I called Jack Ingersoll. He wasn't answering his phone, as usual, but I left a message asking if there was any logical technical explanation for why two folders of my e-mail could be erased and the rest of the computer's workings left intact. I felt certain that the answer was no, but I thought I ought to ask before I called Hogan Jones to report the situation. It seemed pretty obvious to me that somebody had sat down at my desk, opened up my computer and killed those two files, plus my trash can.

But who? Who would have done that? Who could have done that?

Of course, anybody who worked at TenHuis Chocolade could have wandered into the office when I
wasn't there, opened the e-mail program, and killed
anything she wanted to kill. (All our employees are
women.) But she couldn't have done it without being
observed. My office was separated from the shop and
from the workroom only by large panes of glass. It's
a fishbowl. Nobody could go into the office during
business hours without someone noticing.

But if people who worked there would have trouble getting into my computer, it would be even more
difficult for an outsider. Nobody besides the staff
would have any reason to be in my office—or at least
no reason to fool with my computer. If they did, it
would be sure to attract attention from Aunt Nettie
or one of the other hairnet ladies.

The whole thing was nonsense. The missing folders were not important to me. It's not as if I checked
them every morning to see if anything exciting had
turned up. No, I just send stuff, and I don't look at
the sent folder unless I have some question about it.
I simply kill stuff from my incoming mail file, and it
lingers in deleted until I get around to giving the
final commands to kill it forever. I had no idea when
I'd last looked in either file. It had been at least a
month.

Of course, I could figure when the folders had been
emptied. The dates on the handful of remaining
items showed when it had happened.

The two folders had been emptied the day before.
I looked at my calendar and thought back over the
past few days, trying to remember who had been in
my office, who had come into the shop.

I immediately realized that practically everybody I
knew had been there either Tuesday or Wednesday,
including some of the members of the Seventh Food
Group. Jason had come by to tell me about his computer problems. Diane Denham had dropped by to

ask about Lindy and had stayed to complain about
how nosy Julie had been. Of course, Lindy hadn't
been in, because she was home recuperating from
being hit in the head by the thief who'd taken her
laptop. Besides, Lindy was my best and oldest friend.
If I had to suspect Lindy of fooling around with my
computer, or worse, of murder—well, I just couldn't
do it. Carolyn Rose hadn't been into TenHuis Chocolade, but death seemed to take her off the list of
possible villains, too.

Margaret Van Meter had not been in my office that
week either. Did that remove her from the suspect
list? Or make her more likely? That idea seemed silly.
With six kids, Margaret was so homebound she had
trouble finding time to go to the grocery store. Getting out long enough to get into my computer or to
commit murder would have been impossible for her.

Besides, these were all people I knew, people I considered friends. Then I remembered how Hogan
Jones had described them. "These are not friends,"
he'd said. "These are suspects." At that thought I
shivered harder than Martin Schrader had at the idea
of drinking iced tea in January.

But all this had happened a few weeks before Valentine's Day, one of the busiest times of the year for
the chocolate business. Dozens of people had come
into TenHuis Chocolade during the past two days.
Martin Schrader had been in three times, and his
nephew, Brad, had been in once. But I didn't see how
any of these people could have touched my computer unobserved.

Maybe Tracy had seen something. I glanced at the
clock on the workroom wall. She would come to
work in half an hour. I'd ask her.

I wound up spending most of that half hour standing at the counter in the shop. We had a rush of
customers that didn't let up even after Tracy came
in, and both of us had to work the counter until five

thirty. Closing time had come before I had a chance to say anything more to Tracy than, "Please go to the back and bring up a tray of lemon canache bonbons." ("Tangy lemon interior with dark chocolate coating.")

My request for a short chat left Tracy looking as if she'd been called to the principal's office. She perched uneasily on my visitor's chair. "Did I short-change someone?"

"If you did they haven't complained. No, something crazy happened to my computer, and I wondered if anybody had been fooling with it."

"Not me!"

"I'm sure it wasn't you, Tracy. I was wondering about visitors."

"Visitors? Like Brad Schrader?"

"Not him specifically. Anybody. Salesmen. Jason Foster was by yesterday, for example."

"Yes, but he went right in your office. And you were there."

It was hard going. Tracy's job was to mind the counter, not keep an eye on my office. She couldn't remember who had been in it, if I'd been there the whole time the visitors had been, if they'd looked at my computer, or if they'd taken a meat ax to it. Our whole conversation was a waste of time.

After Tracy left I sat and stared at the computer screen. How was I going to figure this out?

The key to the whole mystery was Julie Singletree. It was only after Julie was murdered that the Seventh Food Group began to have trouble with its computers. It was after Julie was murdered that Carolyn was killed, that Lindy was attacked. The whole problem had to hinge on Julie. Who would have wanted to harm her? And why?

I sat looking at that computer screen as if it were a crystal ball, and I were a fortune-teller. I needed to find out more about Julie. How could I do that?

Gradually, an idea formed. I picked up the phone and punched in a number. Joe answered on the second ring.

"Joe, how would you like to have dinner in Holland?"

"If you could wait until around seven, I could get another coat of varnish on this boat. Then you might talk me into it."

"Sounds fine. Then, afterward—I thought we might go by Margaret Van Meter's and look at wedding cakes."

He paused, obviously analyzing what I had said.

So I went on. "Whoever comes to our wedding, they're going to expect cake."

Joe chortled. "You're nosing around, aren't you?"

"It's a dirty job, but somebody's got to do it."

"Okay." Joe sounded resigned. "If I'm going to marry the nosiest woman in west Michigan, I'd better get used to it. I sure don't want you poking around by yourself."

"I'll call Margaret and see if she can talk to us."

Margaret said she should have the youngest kids in bed by eight thirty. "Jim will be home by eight, and he can supervise baths for the boys. So a half hour later should be a good time."

Joe and I barely had time to snag a burger at a popular Holland restaurant. Then he followed my vague directions, and we roamed around until we found Margaret's house.

"What does Jim do?" Joe said as we got out of his truck.

"He works for one of the office furniture suppliers. I think he delivers and assembles."

"He's lucky he's still got a job."

"Right." At one time, our part of Michigan was a center for manufacturing and sales of office furniture, but anybody who reads the newspapers knows that a lot of those companies are closing up operations in our area.

"I can see why Margaret wants to make some money," I said.

Margaret opened the door of the old frame house, smiling her sunny smile and holding a plump, blond baby who wore a blue blanket sleeper. Margaret's hair was pinned up into a knot and dribbles of something stained the front of her sweatshirt. "I kept Teddy up so you could see him," she said.

Joe and I admired the little guy, who Margaret said was ten months old. He grinned at us, showing off four teeth, then coyly buried his face in his mother's neck and peeked at us from under her chin. Two small girls ran to see who had come in and were introduced as Tessa and Marcy. They were two and three, Margaret said. Tessa sucked her thumb and grabbed Margaret's leg, but Marcy came right over to us and batted her eyelashes at Joe like a born flirt. Both wore footed blanket sleepers similar to their baby brother's.

Jim came in from the kitchen then. He was a husky blond guy, the kind who looks as if he could hoist a king-sized steel desk without batting an eye. The baby bottle he held seemed incongruous.

Jim and Joe shook hands; then Jim looked at little Teddy and grinned. "Come on, big guy," he said.

Teddy wriggled all over and made a flying leap out of his mother's arms. I gasped, but Jim caught him expertly and carried him up the stairs. Teddy grabbed the bottle and tipped it back as they went.

"I'll take you guys into the kitchen, if you don't mind," Margaret said. "I laid my sample book out on the table in there. You can look at it while I get the little girls in bed."

She led us through the living room, pausing to introduce us to three little blond boys who were still dressed—James, who was four; Davy, who was six; and Kenneth, who was seven. They were lined up on the couch, watching the Cartoon Network.

The kitchen was outdated in decor, but up-to-date in equipment. In the center was a big oak table. I expected to find that the kids had covered it with something sticky, but it had been scrubbed clean. In fact, Margaret's kitchen would have passed the health department's check with no problem. And the aroma was wonderful in there.

"I put a cake in the oven a few minutes ago," Margaret said. "It's almond flavor. I made a small sample one you can try, if you're interested in that flavor."

"Anything that smells that good, I'll be glad to taste," Joe said.

We sat down at the table and looked at snapshots of Margaret's cakes. I'd described them to Joe as works of art, but he was still surprised by their beauty. And their cost.

"It's the Australian method," I explained. "Or that's what I read in one of Aunt Nettie's magazines. They use a fondant icing, instead of the usual butter cream. And, yes, they're expensive. But they are gorgeous."

We looked at a list of Margaret's flavors for cakes—vanilla, almond, chocolate, strawberry—and the flavors for fillings. That list went on for a whole page. We'd just about settled on almond cake with peach-flavored filling when Margaret came back. She grabbed a small cake out of the oven and tested three larger layers with toothpicks. Then she slid the larger cakes back into the oven and set the timer.

"This little cake will give you an idea of the almond," she said.

"Do you have a wedding tomorrow?" I said.

"Oh, no. I won't use those layers for two weeks. I like to freeze them ahead. They'll keep up to three weeks, and they're a whole lot easier to frost if they're frozen when you do it."

"How about the fondant?"

"I make the flowers ahead. They keep real well, and I can make them at nap time or during the evening. Of course, I have to do the final icing and assembling on the day I deliver the cake."

Then we talked about our wedding cake, and Margaret approved our combination of flavors. "Though I expected you to order chocolate with chocolate frosting," she said. "Will you want a separate groom's cake?"

Joe and I looked at each other. "I think Aunt Nettie is going to do trays of truffles and bonbons instead," I said. "Margaret, this wedding isn't going to be one of your big jobs. It's not a formal do."

"A smaller cake can be beautiful. Do you want it decorated in all white? Or with color?"

"I was thinking of color, but I haven't found a dress yet, and neither has Lindy. And I'll have to pick one before I can decide on a color for the flowers. So I'll have to tell you later."

"I don't have to know until that week." Margaret smiled happily. "I expect your mother will want to have some input, too."

"Joe's mom may," I said. "But I'm deliberately leaving my mom out of the plans. We have fewer arguments that way."

"Smart!"

I was surprised at Margaret's comment, and I must have looked it. So I tried to cover up. "I guess mothers want to have a lot of say."

"My mother did. Our wedding was miserable because of her nagging at us." Margaret smiled. "But we've had a wonderful marriage."

"I can see the two of you are really partners," Joe said. "You'd have to be, to handle these cute kids."

"Jim's just wonderful. He works so hard at the

plant, and after work he goes to the vo-tech center. He's taking a computer repair class."

"You're lucky," I said. "I guess Jim's knowledge has kept you from having all the computer problems the rest of the Seventh Food Group have had."

Margaret began to praise Jim's virus protection programs. I turned my face toward Joe and mouthed a phrase at him. "Go talk to Jim." I only had to do it three times before he blinked, then stood up. "Hey, would Jim mind if I asked him about a computer problem I'm having?"

"Oh, no," Margaret said. "I think he's in the living room. He loves to talk about computers."

As soon as he disappeared through the door, I turned to Margaret. "Listen," I said, "I can't help but believe that all these computer problems, not to mention the killing of Carolyn and the attack on Lindy, are connected to Julie's death."

"All I know is that the police came out and really quizzed me about it all. They looked at our computer for a long time."

"Did they find the e-mails from Julie?"

"No, I don't save that sort of thing. And Jim has me set up so that I don't download from the Net to my computer. He says it's the safest way to stay away from viruses. So unless I do something special, after I've read it, it's gone. So I guess Julie's e-mail to us has just disappeared, unless you . . . ?"

I quickly explained my computer problems. "So I got off lightly, at least so far. I'm glad to hear that the Holland detectives looked into it. Julie herself simply has to be the key to this—well, I guess I'd call it a crime wave. And you were the only one of the Seventh Food Group who knew Julie very well."

Margaret's eyes slid away from mine. "We weren't really very close friends in high school. Then she was away from Holland a long time."

"I know. I talked to her uncle and found out all about the louse she married. But you said she used to come by and see you. What was she really like?"

Margaret shook her head, but she didn't reply.

I pressed on. "Come on, Margaret. Was she a gossip? Was she snobbish? We all found that we'd told her things we didn't intend to tell. Was she genuinely interested in people? Or just even nosier than I am?"

That made Margaret smile a little. "I never knew why she used to come by and see me," she said. "I was glad to see her—sometimes I get so tired of the Disney Channel and three-year-old conversation. But, you're right—I did find that we were talking about things I really didn't want to discuss with her. See, some bad things happened to me in high school. Julie thought I wasn't 'dealing with them.' Whatever that means. She kept telling me I ought to see a counselor, for example. Like I was crazy!"

Margaret turned toward me, and her eyes were full of tears. "As if it were any business of hers how many kids I have!"

"Of course, it wasn't any of her business, Margaret. It sounds as if Julie had read too many self-help books." And Margaret hadn't read enough, I thought. But I kept that to myself.

"Julie definitely had problems of her own," Margaret said. "She was really lonely after she came back to Holland. I guess that's why she bugged me." She blinked hard. "Anyway, Jim says we're not having any more kids. He took steps. And my doctor says seven pregnancies is enough."

Before I could do more than feel slightly startled, Jim's head popped around the kitchen door. "Hey! Are you girls going to share that cake with Joe and me?"

Margaret cut the little almond-flavored cake and put the pieces on plates, then topped it with globs of white frosting she took from the refrigerator. We all went into the living room and ate cake. It was delicious.

Jim turned out to be a pleasant guy, though maybe not one to spend hours discussing philosophy or literature with. Luckily, Joe is willing to discuss mechanical and electronic things, so he kept the conversation rolling.

My brain was still bouncing around with the information Margaret had let slip. I nearly blew it as Joe and I went out the door. "The kids are absolutely darling," I said. "I'm so glad we got to see them all."

"All is right," Jim said. "Six is plenty!"

"I hope you two will want to have kids," Margaret said. "I couldn't live without mine."

I tried to be noncommittal. "We're pretty old to have a big family. Anyway, Margaret, thanks for putting us down for a cake. I'll let you know more details ASPG."

Three sets of eyes stared at me blankly. "ASPG?" Margaret said.

I'd done it again. "ASAP!" I said. "As soon as possible. As soon I find a dress and settle on flowers."

Joe rolled his eyes. "Come on, Lee," he said. "No more almond extract for you."

Everybody laughed—even me—and Joe and I climbed into his truck.

"Gosh, Joe," I said. "Margaret let something slip. First she said 'some bad things' happened to her in high school. Then she said she's had seven pregnancies. Six kids, but seven pregnancies. Do you think she had an abortion? Or gave a baby up for adoption?"

"That's a pretty broad speculation, Lee. She could have had a miscarriage since she and Jim were married."

"I don't know when she would have found time,

with a kid every year. But it's possible, I guess. Oh, gee! An out-of-wedlock pregnancy would be about the worst thing that could happen to a girl who went to Holland Christian."

"I'm sure she wouldn't have been the first case they had, even at Holland Christian. But if you want to link her up with Julie and Carolyn's deaths—well, that's pretty far-fetched. With all these kids, and only two of them in school, I don't see how she could be racing down to Warner Pier to destroy computers and attack florists."

"You're right. I didn't consider her a possibility to begin with, and after seeing her kids and how busy they keep her—I think I can forget Margaret. Besides, she doesn't have the right skill set."

"On the other hand," Joe said, "Jim has exactly the right skill set. He could have done everything that's been done without breaking a sweat."

Chapter 15

Joe was right, of course. In thinking of Margaret as Margaret—singular—I'd been ignoring the fact that she had a partner: Jim.

And Jim had all the skills the killer of Julie and Carolyn would have needed. He was strong enough to bash effectively. He undoubtedly knew Julie, so she would have let him into her apartment. He hadn't known Carolyn, or I didn't think he had, but if he'd identified himself as Margaret's husband, she wouldn't have hesitated to turn her back on him. As a delivery guy for an office furniture company, he probably had a company truck and unlimited opportunity to roam around west Michigan doing anything he wanted to. All he had to do was tell his boss that the day's delivery and assembly chores had taken longer than expected. He might have to disconnect the odometer on the delivery truck, but I had a feeling Jim could manage that with his eyes closed.

Plus, Jim apparently had specialized computer knowledge, gained as he tried to learn a skill that might lead to a higher-paying job. True, he was studying the electronic aspects of computers—the stuff that required a screwdriver—but I was willing to bet he could handle a little light hacking.

As for motive, Jim seemed to be devoted to Margaret. If he had felt that Julie threatened Margaret, he might have decided to take care of that threat permanently.

By the time I'd analyzed the situation, the cab of Joe's truck was warmed up, but I gave a violent shiver anyway. Joe reached over and took my hand. "Rabbit run over your grave?"

"It's awful, Joe. Awful to be suspicious of people you know, people you consider friends."

"I think that's one reason Hogan keeps trying to warn you not to be so curious, Lee. When either he or the Holland cops make an arrest, you're going to feel better if you can say, 'Oh, I never dreamed he was the one,' than if you had some part in piling up the evidence."

I considered that. Then I rejected it. "But I'm in regular contact with people who appear to be mixed up in these killings," I said. "I'm placed in a position where I can pick up things that Hogan and the Holland detectives can't. And because of that, things I may say innocently could be misconstrued. What if, for example, I said something like, 'Oh, Aunt Nettie got the biggest laugh out of that joke you sent on the Tuesday e-mail,' and what if I said it to the wrong person? It might accidentally put Aunt Nettie in danger."

"But nosing around may put *you* in danger, Lee. And that upsets me a lot."

I unhooked my seat belt, moved to the center of the pickup, and put my head on Joe's shoulder. "I try not to be completely stupid."

He kissed my forehead. "Then buckle up," he said.

"Darling! You really care about me!"

After we'd both chuckled—and I'd fastened the center seat belt—Joe spoke again. "So what's your next move?"

"My whole object is to get to know what Julie was really like. Her death started this whole chain of events, and it seems logical that her character inspired it in some way. The Seventh Food Group is involved—how I don't understand. So I want to talk to each member and find out what he or she thought about Julie."

"That makes sense."

"I thought Julie was pretty innocuous, myself. But I find that she had managed to alienate most of the other members of the group with her amateur psychologist act. She 'outed' Jason and his partner, Ross, to Ross's dad. She apparently knew about something unfortunate that had happened to Margaret in high school and kept trying to get her to 'deal with it.' This might have meant she threatened to tell someone else something that Margaret, or Margaret and Jim, didn't want them to know."

"So what's next?"

"So now I wonder what she did to the Denhams. They certainly weren't wholehearted fans of Julie Singletree."

Joe sighed. "When can we go see them?"

"You don't need to go."

"You're not going alone!"

"Actually, I was planning to see them in a group. The whole Seventh Food Group. We've all been invited to a preview of a closeout sale at Veldkamp Used Food Equipment and Supply tomorrow night. According to the e-mails, everybody's going. Maybe I can talk to Ronnie and Diane informally there. But I won't be alone. I'll stick close to either Lindy or Aunt Nettie."

The person I was to stick close to turned out to be Lindy, because Aunt Nettie decided not to go to the Veldkamp sale. I couldn't decide if she wanted an evening alone with Hogan—she did ask him over to dinner—or if she wanted me to make more decisions about TenHuis Chocolade on my own. It may have been both, but the evening with Hogan probably carried the most weight.

So Lindy and I went alone, and Lindy insisted on driving her bright green compact, despite her injury just two days earlier. "I feel fine," she said. "I guess it takes more than a whack up side the head to slow me down. The only thing that might make me nervous about picking you up is that place on Lake Shore Drive where the bank's caving in."

"The street department has a barricade up," I said. "Not that it would stop anything heavier than a bicycle."

"But at least I'll be able to tell the spot where I want to stay away from the edge. Now, Lee, you be sure to wear your warmest coat. I can guarantee that Veldkamp's warehouse is going to be as cold as a well-digger's fanny."

Lindy was right. We entered Veldkamp's through the heated showroom, but once we were escorted to the cavernous warehouse, we might as well have been in Santa's shipping department. I'd worn my wooly white hat and scarf, my red down jacket, my fur-lined boots, a pair of flannel-lined jeans, and long johns, and I had no impulse to unzip, unhat, or otherwise remove or loosen any garment I had on. Not only was it physically cold, the decor featured concrete floors, dim lights, huge cardboard cartons, gigantic black ranges, and stainless steel appliances in jumbo sizes. Not cozy. It would have felt cold in there on the hottest day of July.

The Seventh Food Group members were obviously not the only people who'd been invited to preview the closeout sale offerings. There were around fifty people roaming around, checking out plate warmers and kicking the tires of rolling tables. Lindy started looking for a freezer. I remembered that I'd promised Joe I'd stick close to her, but Veldkamp's warehouse didn't seem all that dangerous, despite the big equipment that could have hidden a regiment of mad bombers. I found a Veldkamp employee and asked directions to the cooling tunnel.

A cooling tunnel is a little air conditioner for chocolates. It's open at both ends and a conveyor belt runs through it, passing under a Plexiglas arch; cold air sprays into that miniature tunnel. Chocolate melts easily—that's why you can't hold it in your hand very long without having sticky fingers. So chocolatiers can mold it or dip it readily, but they then have to let it get cool before they can do a next step, such as adding another layer of chocolate. A cooling tunnel speeds this process up.

Aunt Nettie had explained what I should look for in a cooling tunnel and how much I should be willing to pay. The one Veldkamp's had looked pretty good— or it would once we'd cleaned it to Aunt Nettie standards—so I put in a written bid. Then I moved to the stainless steel section and began to look at work tables and rolling storage racks.

All the time I was keeping an eye out for Diane and Ronnie Denham, or I thought I was. So I don't know why I jumped about a foot when I rolled a six-foot-tall storage rack aside and came face to face with Diane.

"Oh!" I said. "You startled me."

Diane smiled her cheerful Mrs. Claus smile. She was bundled up in a long blue down coat and had a plaid wool scarf wrapped around her head. Just a few of her beautiful white curls peeked out over her forehead. "Hi, Lee. What are you looking for?"

"Storage racks and work tables for Aunt Nettie." I'd already decided to forget subtlety and simply to ask for information from Diane, so I plunged right in. "I was also looking for a chance to talk to you."

"What about?"

"Julie."

Diane looked away from me. She put out a gloved hand and gently rolled a stainless steel rack back and forth. "Aren't the police looking into Julie's death?"

"Of course. I'm not interested in her death. I'm interested in her life. All sorts of bad things have happened to the Seventh Food Group since Julie was killed. I have a feeling that's because of things that happened while she was alive. I barely knew Julie, but I feel compelled to—well, get to know her posthaste. I mean, posthumously!"

Diane ignored my slip of the tongue. "I only met her a few times."

"That's what all of us say. But she managed to elevate—I mean, alienate!—at least half the members of the Seventh Food Group with her amateur psychology."

"I didn't know that."

"I just figured it out this week. Jason—this is just an example—she urged Jason and Ross to open up about their relationship with Ross's dad. Jason says the poor old guy is ninety years old and in a nursing home. Until Julie shot her mouth off, he considered Jason merely a friend of his son's. What good is it going to do for them to confront him with their relationship at this point in his life?"

Diane shook her head. "It wouldn't be kind at all, and it wouldn't affect Jason and Ross, either."

"Exactly! But I have a feeling that Julie was Little Miss Helpful to everybody she was around. I know she tried to talk to me about my divorce. I had a hard time dodging her. Did she give you and Ronnie the same treatment? What did you all think of her?"

Diane's face crumpled, and she turned away. "Julie was awfully nosy," she said. "She went way beyond asking personal questions. She had—well, she'd researched us on the Internet. I think she'd researched all of us."

"All of us?"

"Yes. But it was strange, Lee. She didn't offer to tell us anything about anyone else. About Jason, for example, or about you or any of the others. When you called her an 'amateur psychologist,' that described it. She thought everybody should put all their problems on display, should forget about keeping anything secret."

I shuddered. "I guess she simply hadn't gotten to me yet. I have as many secrets as anybody else. But she kept her own life completely secret."

Diane caught her breath sharply, and I realized she was looking at something behind me. I looked around and saw Ronnie coming toward us.

Diane leaned toward me. When she spoke again, she had dropped her voice almost to a whisper. "Lee, don't talk about Julie in front of Ronnie. In fact, there's no point in talking about this at all. We signed a confidentiality agreement. We cannot say a word. Under penalty of law."

I snapped my gaping mouth shut just as Ronnie joined us. "Hi, Lee," he said. "Diane, there's a set of big mixing bowls over there you might want to take a look at."

They went away, and I strolled aimlessly among the giant cartons and superduper mixers while I thought about what Diane had said. A confidentiality agreement? What was that exactly? Under what situation would an outwardly ordinary couple like the Denhams sign such a thing? The settlement of a lawsuit? Something to do with a juvenile offender?

It was a question for a lawyer. I resolved to ask Joe. Then I wandered back to the rolling racks and picked a couple out that I thought would suit Aunt Nettie. TenHuis Chocolade uses a lot of those racks—stainless steel gizmos on wheels, each around six feet tall and three feet square, with space for two dozen metal trays that slide in and out of metal supports. We could use a half dozen, Aunt Nettie had told me, but we had no place to put that many.

Was TenHuis going to have to expand? If we decided I needed an assistant, we'd need a place for him or her to work, and Aunt Nettie definitely could use more storage space. But where would we find the room? I tucked that idea away to think about after I'd figured out Julie.

Lindy and I left for Warner Pier about nine o'clock. She'd made arrangements for Mike to look over the freezer. I was mostly silent as she drove home; Lindy was mad at one of the teachers at Warner Pier Elementary, and I heard about her for the whole thirty miles, but I only listened to about half of it.

It wasn't until she had turned the green compact onto the Warner River Bridge that she said something that really caught my ear.

"You know, Lee, that car's been behind us all the way from Holland."

I twisted around to see the headlights of the car behind us. "Are you sure?"

"Not absolutely positive, of course, but I first noticed a set of headlights that shape and size just as we stopped at the Twenty-fourth Street light."

"Why didn't you say something earlier?"

"I didn't think anything of it until the lights followed us through Warner Pier. And now he's closing up on us."

"Should you turn around and go back?"

"To the police station? There's nobody there this time of night. They close up and let the county dispatcher take calls."

"We could go to the Stop and Shop. It's open all night."

"Yeah, and some old guy's at the cash register. A lot of help he would be."

"He could call Tony or Joe. Heck, I've got my cell

phone. I can call Tony or Joe. Or the cops." I reached for my purse.

"I've got another idea, Lee. Why don't I pull in a driveway and turn around. We can go back to town. If the car doesn't follow us—well, I'm going to feel pretty dumb if we call Tony or Joe, and it turns out to be somebody who lives farther on down Lake Shore Drive coming back from the Holland Multiplex."

The interstate coming down from Holland had been well plowed, of course, and thousands of cars had driven down it since the last snow, beating the pavement almost free of snow and ice. In contrast, Lake Shore Drive was barely two lanes wide, and it had only local traffic, so it had snow piled along the edges. But there were lots of driveways, roads, and lanes branching off it.

"Turn in at the Nolans' house," I said. "Where the big hedge is. If you cut the lights, it ought to hide us."

Lindy nodded. She sped up, wheeling around a curve in the road. I was looking back at the car behind us when she suddenly turned off the headlights, and I felt the compact swerve as she cut the wheels sharply right.

"Hang on," Lindy said.

Then she hit the brakes. My seat belt snapped, keeping me immobile. I kept looking out the back window. I could see a red reflection on the Nolans' hedge. "Foot off the brakes!" I said.

The red disappeared, as did a fainter white. Lindy had turned off the ignition.

For a moment I was scared that the car following us would come into the Nolans' drive right after us. Then where would we be? Caught between a hedge and a hard place.

But the lights went on by. The car behind us wasn't even driving very fast.

"Could you see what kind of car it was?" I said.

"I wouldn't recognize it if I saw it. The headlights

just looked odd. But it sure didn't look like a madman trying to run us off the road, did it?"

"No. But let's drive back to town anyway."

Lindy started the car, backed out of the drive, and headed back the way we'd come. I kept a close watch, but no car was behind us. It was close to ten o'clock by then, and all the residents of Lake Shore Drive had apparently gone home. We saw lights through the bare branches of the trees, but we were the only car moving. We drove back across the Warner River Bridge and into town, and Lindy pulled into the parking lot that overlooked the bridge. Again she cut her lights.

"Unless our eyes are reflecting," I said, "we should be hard to see."

"We'll have to peek through our fingers if he comes back."

He didn't come back. We sat there looking at the bridge for ten minutes and not a single vehicle crossed it, either coming toward us or going away.

After a few minutes Lindy began to laugh. "I won't tell Joe about this, if you won't tell Tony."

"I do feel pretty stupid. But considering that you were actually attacked just a couple of days ago . . ."

"That was just a thief." Lindy's voice was firm. "I refuse to worry about this any more. I'm driving you home."

We laughed and giggled all the way across the bridge. The relief was great. But I couldn't help peeking out the back window now and then. So I saw the headlights first.

I gasped. A car had pulled out of a driveway and turned the same way we were traveling. It was moving fast; it fishtailed as it turned onto Lake Shore Drive.

"Not again!" Lindy said.

"Maybe it's not the same guy."

"They look like the same headlights to me," she

said. "They reflect off that grill in the middle, and that grill looks like long teeth. Let's move!"

The little car took a leap forward. Lake Shore Drive follows the edge of Lake Michigan. It's a narrow blacktop road, and there was ice and snow along the edges. Not a good place for fast driving. But I didn't care, and Lindy apparently didn't either. She gunned the motor.

The car behind us was closing in. I didn't say anything, since Lindy could see it coming in the rearview mirror. I wanted her to concentrate on driving, not looking at the strange headlights behind us.

Lindy didn't panic. When she spoke, her voice was calm. "Where's that place where the bank's eaten away?"

"About a quarter of a mile farther on."

"I guess I could hit the brakes and try to make a U-turn."

"Then he could hit us broadside."

No, going on seemed to be our only choice. Lindy goosed the car, and it responded with more speed.

The car that was following us came closer. It came right up on the back bumper. Then it suddenly cut left, as if it were going to pass us. But instead it drove along beside us. But it wasn't moving parallel to us. It was edging closer to us, ready to sideswipe the car.

Then I saw orange in the headlights. "There's the barricade! He's going to try to push us over!"

Lindy's response probably saved our lives. She threw on her brakes.

Instantly the car beside us shot ahead.

Our tires hit a patch of ice, and the compact went into a spin, but we didn't hit the guy who had been chasing us. We had almost come to a stop when the car slid slowly into the wooden barricade. Moving almost in slow motion, we went over the bank backward, sliding down toward Lake Michigan.

Chapter 16

I thought we were going to die. I knew how steep that drop was: straight down. And I knew how far it was: at least forty feet. And I knew what was at the bottom: the shallows of Lake Michigan, frozen solid. I expected us to plummet, hit hard, and be crushed to death as the car folded up like an accordion.

But it didn't happen that way. We didn't plummet; we slid gently. We didn't fall straight down; my feet were as high as my shoulders, true, but it was more like gradually tipping over backward in a kitchen chair than like a beach stone splashing into the water.

We hit the ice at the edge of Lake Michigan with a crash, but the car didn't fold up like an accordion. It bounced. It seemed to be all in one piece, and was even sitting fairly level. The motor was still purring, the lights were still on, and the heater fan was still blowing hot air.

And we had stopped moving.

"Lindy! Are you okay?"

"I think so! Are *you* okay?"

"I'm conscious, and nothing seems to be broken. Can you get out of the car?"

"Is that a good idea?"

"It might catch fire."

Lindy punched dashboard buttons. The headlights went out, and the heater fan fell silent. "That will make it harder for that guy to find us, if he comes back," she said.

"I wish we could get out of the car without turning on the interior lights, but we can't. So we'd better hurry."

Hurrying did not turn out to be an option. Lindy's door was jammed shut. Snow and ice were piled up outside my door as well, and it took me several hard shoves to get it open. Then Lindy couldn't find her hat. Refusing to leave the car without a hat didn't seem dumb right at that moment. The temperature was in the teens. I was sure grateful that we were both warmly dressed.

Once she found her hat, Lindy had to climb over the center console. She did a belly whopper onto the ice to get out my door. We were panting by the time we both were standing on the passenger's side of the car, hanging onto the door as if it were our last connection with solid ground. The footing was terrible, since the car was surrounded by clumps and clods and splinters of ice. The lake occasionally freezes smoothly, but crashing a car into it had thrown up all sorts of icy debris, regardless of how smooth the ice had been when we hit.

At least there was no open water. We didn't have to leap from floe to floe. Instead, we went toward the high bank we'd just slid down, stepping carefully and hanging onto each other as if we had Velcro on our gloves. We couldn't tell when we got onto the shore, actually. The chunks of ice seemed to go right up the bank, and I *knew* there had to be some beach someplace under the snow.

"Can we get up the bank?" Lindy asked.

"What if that guy is up there waiting?" I gestured to the right and toward the top of the bank. "There's a house up there with the lights still on. Maybe we can climb up."

We started walking. It's a miracle neither of us broke a leg. Of course, it wasn't too dark. Even when the moon is behind clouds, a layer of snow gives the terrain a sort of glow, so we could see a bit. Lindy began to mutter because she hadn't thought to grab her flashlight from the glove box. That reminded me that I had picked up my purse, and there was a penlight on my key chain. We used it occasionally, but mostly we walked over the chunky ice that covered the beach using the moonlight filtered through clouds and reflected from snow.

Then we heard a man's voice shouting, "Hello! Who's there?"

I put the penlight out, and Lindy and I stood still, clutching each other.

Lindy whispered. "Do you think it's the guy who ran us off the road?"

I whispered back. "He probably wouldn't yell. So it's likely to be whoever lives in that house. We'd better chance it."

I turned the penlight back on and waved it. Then I yelled,. "Hello! We had a wreck! The car went over the edge!"

"Anybody hurt?"

"Not bad! How can we get up the bank?"

"My stairs are a little further along. I'll go get a ladder!"

Our rescuer turned out to be a retired gentleman named Oscar Patterson. I had never met him, but I'd noticed his mailbox, and I sure was glad to make his acquaintance. Like most of the houses on the Lake Michigan side of Lake Shore Drive, his home had a wooden stairway that led down to the beach. The bottom section had been taken down for the winter, so the ice wouldn't grind it into splinters, but he brought a ladder, and we were able to climb it to reach the first landing. After that, it was merely a matter of inching our way up, stair by snowy and icy stair, hanging onto the wooden handrail.

"I've been telling 'em someone was going to go over back there," our rescuer said. "I called the street department. They said nothing could be done until they could get hold of some more of those barricades. Now maybe they'll put up something stouter. Too late. As usual."

The next hour was full of events. Mr. Patterson and his wife clucked over us. We called people—Aunt Nettie and Hogan, Joe, and Tony. They all came rushing over, and our rescuers' driveway became packed with cars.

My biggest question was how we had avoided being killed. I was sure we'd gone over a real cliff, and by rights we should have been crushed to death.

But Hogan said we'd missed the steepest spot. "You went off about fifteen feet before the place where the road has been eaten away," he said. "It was a steep slope, but you slid down at a forty-five-degree angle, not a ninety. You were damn lucky."

"Thank God Lindy hit the brakes when she did," I said.

We had to tell Hogan the whole story. His biggest concern was that neither of us could describe the car that had pushed us off the road. Our vague description of its headlights was not a lot of help, though Lindy swore the car's grill had looked like monstrous teeth.

Other than scrapes and bruises, neither Lindy nor I seemed to be hurt, and the men in our respective lives took us home just as the wrecker arrived. I was sure glad to see my own bed, though I can't claim that I slept very well. One moment I was so grateful to be alive that I couldn't close an eye, and the next I was so puzzled as to who would have tried to push Lindy and me over that steep bank that I just lay in bed with my brain whizzing around.

Maybe the biggest puzzle was simply which of us he'd been out to get. I couldn't see any reason for either of us to attract the attention of a killer. Anyway, I mulled it over most of the night; I guess it was more comforting to do that than to remember what a close escape we'd had.

I finally fell asleep around five o'clock. Aunt Nettie must have tiptoed out, because I didn't wake up until ten a.m. Then I panicked. Even though it was Saturday, TenHuis Chocolade was keeping regular business hours, getting ready for the big holiday. I was late.

By the time I'd showered, dressed, and gone by the police station to sign a statement, it was noon. So I came in the door of TenHuis Chocolade in something of a tizzy. I couldn't afford to take a half day off, not even because I'd had a narrow escape followed by a sleepless night.

Dolly Jolly was working the front counter. "Hi, Lee!" she shouted. "Heard you had an exciting night! I'm assigned up here for the day! Nettie called Hazel in, asked her to fill the gap this week!"

I gave a sigh of relief. Hazel had formerly been Aunt Nettie's second-in-command. She'd retired two months earlier after her husband, Harry, suffered a stroke.

"If Harry can spare her, we can really use her help," I told Dolly. Then I went back to tell Hazel I was glad to see her.

Harry, she said, was doing better. Their son would be visiting for the next week. "It won't hurt him to take his dad to physical therapy," she said, "and it won't hurt Harry if he has to depend on somebody besides me for a few days." I thought her mouth looked a little grim, but I didn't ask for details.

I went to my desk, vowing to concentrate on the chocolate business all afternoon. At first I found this difficult, since the phone kept ringing. I knew it would mostly be friends calling to commiserate over the wreck, but it could be a customer, so I didn't dare not answer. The calls from friends made it hard to get anything done; they kept Julie's and Carolyn's deaths, the attack on Lindy, and the harrowing slide into Lake Michigan bouncing around in my brain. But about four o'clock something happened that focused my attention on TenHuis Chocolade in a big way.

The phone rang. Again. I tried not to sigh as I answered. "TenHuis Chocolade."

"Hello." It was a male voice, and it sounded young. And it didn't say anything more.

So I spoke again. "Can I help you?"

"Well . . . This is Bob Vanderheide. Is Aunt— Could I speak to Mrs. TenHuis, please?"

For a moment my mind was a complete blank. Bob Vanderheide? I should know that name. Then I remembered. It was Aunt Nettie's nephew. The one whose mother had written about his job prospects.

I decided to be friendly. "Bobby!" I said. "Hello! Aunt Nettie's in the black. I mean the back! In the workroom. I'll have to go get her. This is Lee McKinney."

"Oh, hi." Bobby didn't sound enthusiastic. "I guess we're cousins."

"Shirttail cousins. No blood relation. How are you?"

"Fine."

The conversation was not going anywhere. I told Bobby—or Bob—I'd find Aunt Nettie, put the phone down, and went back to the workroom. Aunt Nettie wasn't there. I checked the break room. Not there. The restroom door was open, so I peeked inside. No sign of her there either. Finally, I asked Hazel. Aunt Nettie, she said, had gone to the Superette for four quarts of whipping cream. So I'd have to handle Bobby—I mean, Bob—myself.

I headed back to the office. "Aunt Nettie stepped out for a few minutes. Give me your number, and I'll have her call you."

"No!" Bob paused again. "Listen, tell her that I need to be over on that side of Michigan on Monday, and I'll try to come by. Okay?"

"Sure. She'll want you to stay over, Bob."

"I better plan to drive back that night."

"I'll tell her. But we have plenty of room, and she'd love to have you stay."

"I just need to talk to her. I'll see her Monday afternoon." He hung up.

Oh, rats! Just what I needed. My rival heir was appearing.

I scolded myself for feeling that way about Bobby—I mean Bob. But I did. He was a blood relative to Aunt Nettie. I wasn't. He might end up owning TenHuis Chocolade.

Well, I wouldn't be working for *him*. No matter what happened. I could find another job. I could commute into Holland or Grand Rapids. I could scrub floors, wash dishes, or clean toilets.

My mental tirade was interrupted by Hazel, who put her head in my door and said Aunt Nettie was back. "Did you want something important?"

"Tell her that her nephew Bobby—I mean, Bob—called and said he'll be by to see her Monday afternoon."

"Oh, that's nice." Hazel smiled and went back to the workroom.

Nice. Hazel said Bobby's visit would be nice. I addressed myself to the computer screen and adjusted my attitude.

Hazel was right, of course. Aunt Nettie would be pleased to see Bob. I was acting like a jealous little girl, afraid my favorite aunt would ignore me for another child, one who was younger and possibly cuter. I'd better straighten up, or Aunt Nettie would be perfectly entitled to disinherit me.

I was able to laugh at the idea that I'd be cleaning toilets if Bobby took over TenHuis Chocolade. After all, I had a degree in accounting and a lot of job experience. I wasn't down to cleaning toilets yet. There was even the possibility that Bob would turn out to be a really smart guy who would be an asset to TenHuis Chocolade.

I was about to log on and check my e-mail when the next interruption came. My friend Barbara, the banker, came in. She had to hear all about the accident and the miraculous escape Lindy and I had had. I had to repeat the whole story. But it was only ten minutes before Barbara got up, ready to head back to the bank.

"I'm awfully glad you two made it out in one piece," she said. "Where had you been?"

I reported on our trip to Holland in an absent-minded way, because Barbara's question had triggered a memory. One of my main purposes in going to the Veldkamp sales preview had been to quiz Diane and Ronnie Denham. I hadn't learned a lot from Diane, but she had said one provocative thing. Diane had told me she felt sure that Julie had looked all of the Seventh Food Group up on the Internet.

I doubted that there was anything about me on the Internet, but her comment had made me wonder if there wasn't something about the Denhams there. My old curiosity bump began itching madly. I connected to the Internet and looked up their names.

At first I didn't find a thing. There was only one mention of "Ronnie" or "Ronald" or "Diane" named Denham on the Internet. That mention listed them as proprietors of the Hideaway Inn. Then I checked the Warner Pier Chamber of Commerce membership list. Diane, I learned, had a middle initial. A minute later I struck pay dirt.

In another state, clear across the country, a guidance counselor named "D. B. Denham" had blown the whistle on a scheme her principal had worked out, a scheme which misappropriated a local foundation's scholarship funds. The local newspaper's stories on the scandal were indexed on the Internet, and so were the stories run by a major newspaper in the state.

I didn't have time to read all the stories, so I skipped to the end of the index. And I came up quite frustrated. The stories ended abruptly with an out-of-court settlement that was not revealed. Hmmm.

I looked back at a couple of the news items, and I began to read between the lines. The school board had been covering up like mad. The erring principal had been fired, true, but not before he had persecuted—that's not too strong a word—the whistleblower. The whistleblower, this D. B. Denham, had finally sued the principal and the school board because of the persecution and the board's failure to stop it. The school board, which had clearly been in the wrong, had been forced into an out-of-court settlement. D. B. Denham had accepted the settlement, signed an agreement not to reveal any more details about the case publicly, and taken early retirement.

"And bought a B&B in Warner Pier, Michigan," I said. "Hmmm."

No wonder Diane had resented Julie nosing into their affairs. If her connection with the case had made the papers, it would have endangered her settlement.

The phone had rung two more times while I was checking the Internet—one friend and one customer—and now it rang again. I didn't even bother to sigh before I picked up the receiver.

"TenHuis Chocolade."

"Is this Lee McKinney?" It was the voice of a woman. It didn't sound young, but it sounded firm.

"Yes. May I help you?"

"I hope so. This is Rachel Schrader. I'm going to be at the Warner Pier cottage tomorrow, and I'm hoping you can come to see me there."

CHOCOLATE CHAT

QUOTATIONS FROM BRILLAT-SAVARIN

Anthelme Brillat-Savarin was a French lawyer and gastronome who wrote extensively on food, drink and gracious living in the early nineteenth century. Naturally, he had several things to say about chocolate. Chocolate was then almost exclusively a drink.

"If one swallows a cup of chocolate only three hours after a copious lunch, everything will be perfectly digested and there will still be room for dinner."

"It has been shown as proof positive that carefully prepared chocolate is as healthful a food as it is pleasant; that it is nourishing and easily digested . . . That it is above all helpful to people who must do a great deal of mental work.

"If any man has drunk a little too deeply from the cup of physical pleasure, if he has spent too much time at his desk that should have been spent asleep, if his fine spirits have become temporarily dulled; if he finds the air too damp, the minutes too slow, the atmosphere too heavy to withstand, if he is obsessed with a fixed idea which bars him from any freedom of thought, if he is any of these poor creatures, we say, let him be given a good pint of amber-flavored chocolate and marvels will be performed."

Chapter 17

Stunned amazement swept over me. Rachel Schrader? The grande dame of western Michigan? She wanted me to come to see her? I was dumbstruck, so when I was finally able to speak, naturally I said something dumb.

"Mrs. Shatter? I mean, Mrs. Schrader! Of course, I'll be happy to meet with you. What . . . ?"

I stopped in the middle of my question. I couldn't think just how to ask Rachel Schrader what the hell she wanted.

I might be confused, but Mrs. Schrader wasn't. "Naturally, Ms. McKinney, you're wondering what my business is, and how it concerns you. I'm calling because we are beginning to dispose of Julie's belongings, and I want to ask your help."

"My help? I mean, of course I'll be glad to help."

"I've always read the Warner Pier weekly newspaper, just because I own property near there. And last week I happened to note that the chamber of commerce is sponsoring a drive to collect clothing and household goods to benefit the women's shelter."

"Yes. It's one of our ongoing projects."

"Martin told me you were serving on the chamber board. I'd love for Julie's things to benefit abused women. If you wouldn't mind helping me by delivering them . . ."

"Of course, Mrs. Schrader. But—"

She didn't let me finish my sentence. "In addition, this will give me an opportunity to have a chat with the granddaughter of my old friend."

Her invitation was a royal command. I couldn't argue, though I did tell her TenHuis Chocolade would be open, even though the next day was a Sunday. Mrs. Schrader gave me two phone numbers— the Warner Pier house and her cell phone—in case I was going to run late. We agreed to meet at eleven o'clock.

I was still amazed as I hung up, and I headed straight back to the workroom. I felt sure Aunt Nettie would understand what was so peculiar about Rachel Schrader's request.

I tried to tell her about that request in simple terms, not imposing my own amazement. I wanted Aunt Nettie's honest reaction. And after I told her, I found it satisfying to see her eyes grow wide and even more satisfying to hear what she said.

"That's the oddest thing I ever heard of."

"That's what I thought," I said.

"Doesn't Mrs. Schrader realize that the women's shelter is *in* Holland? Why would she go to Holland, load Julie's things up, and bring them to Warner Pier to give them to the chamber drive? Some chamber person will have to load them up and carry them back to Holland."

"It would certainly be a lot easier to do it directly."

"Unless she thinks the chamber benefits in some way."

"Like winning a contest? She said she had seen the

story about the drive in the *Warner Pier Gazette*. And that story made it quite clear that we were trying to benefit the shelter, not gain any benefit ourselves."

Aunt Nettie nodded. "So her request is obviously just an excuse. She wants to talk to you, Lee. Why?"

"That's the question. If she wants to talk to me, why take this indirect method? Why not just call me up and talk? I certainly would get together with Rachel Schrader any time of the day or night, on the phone or in person. Why does she feel she needs an excuse to ask me to come to see her?"

Aunt Nettie and I shrugged and shook our heads in unison. Neither of us had an answer.

"Take her a pound of chocolates," Aunt Nettie said. "And at least you'll get a look at that house. It's supposed to be a real showplace."

I decided to keep seeing the house as my goal and to quit trying to anticipate what in the world Rachel Schrader wanted. Whatever it was, worrying wasn't going to help me figure it out. And it would be fun to see the Schrader house. Joe had pointed it out to me from the lakeside. From the water it looked like a flying saucer, if a flying saucer could be made of glass, floating in for a gentle landing on top of the dunes. Yes, it would be interesting to see the revolutionary structure up close.

So at ten forty-five the next day I headed for the south edge of Warner Pier and turned into the nondescript entrance to the Schrader property. I'd had to ask Aunt Nettie how to get there from Lake Shore Drive. There was certainly nothing of the showplace about the entrance.

Except the paving. Around Warner Pier, as in most rural neighborhoods, ordinary property owners have drives surfaced with sand or gravel. The Schrader driveway—naturally it had been cleared of snow— was asphalt. I will say that it was a one-way drive, quite narrow, but it was asphalt. The asphalt didn't cover a short drive, either. That drive stretched toward the lakeshore, disappearing into the woods as it curved to the right.

On the first curve was a small wooden house. It wasn't made of logs, but it had natural wood siding, and I was immediately sure it was the "cabin" that Brad Schrader had described. A Prius, a combination electric-gasoline car, had been backed into an open shed at the side. So I gathered that Brad was home, though I didn't see any sign of life as I drove by.

The road went on, passing through thick woods. Giant trees—some with bare branches and some evergreens—towered overhead. The snow on the ground was lumpy; young trees and other undergrowth would cover the ground in spring.

The woods were lovely. I could see why Mike Herrera was eager to find out what the family's plans for the site were. Judging by the length of the road into it, the property was several hundred acres in size—maybe more. And it ran along the lakeshore. With woods and beach, the property had everything to make it a fantastic nature preserve. On the other hand, it would also make a great site for a resort—if the right zoning could be arranged. I didn't know which Mike thought would benefit Warner Pier the most.

After driving what seemed like three miles, but which was probably under a tenth of that, I saw the glint of glass through the trees. I rounded a final curve and drew up before a dramatic house.

If the house looked like a flying saucer from the lake, from the land it looked like an egg—a brown egg. It was oval and apparently made of cast concrete painted a medium tan. But it was built in a strictly symmetrical design. A door—carved and painted black—was smack in the middle of the front façade. The door was flanked by broad floor-to-ceiling windows. Even broader expanses of concrete stretched

out beyond the windows, forming an arc that reflected the shape of the six broad stone steps that led
from the drive. Matching concrete planters curved
around the steps. I suppose they held plants in warm
weather, but now they were full of rounded humps.
A closer look showed me that lake stones the size
and shape of ostrich eggs were peeking through the
snow here and there.

I parked and got out of the van, bringing the box
of chocolates Aunt Nettie had sent. Apparently Rachel Schrader had told her staff I was coming, because the carved black door opened immediately,
and an attractive gray-haired woman wearing a
white pants suit came out.

The woman gave me a welcoming smile, which
displayed deep dimples. She spoke in a strained,
high-pitched voice. "Ms. McKinney? Please come in."

She ushered me into the house. "I'm Hilda Van-
Til," she said. "Mrs. Schrader's aide. She's out in
the overlook."

Ms. VanTil took my coat and hat, and as she was
hanging them up I got a glimpse of a control panel
that must have powered a fancy security system.
Then she led me through a foyer and a living room,
both filled with the kind of completely unadorned
furniture that costs the earth. The simple rooms could
have seemed cold, but they didn't. The furniture,
flooring, and walls were warm colors—corals, rusts,
deep browns—and the textures were nubby and
wooly and comforting. The few pieces of art—giant
paintings and imposing sculpture—were strikingly
displayed.

The room beyond was another story. Ms. VanTil
had called it "the overlook," and that was a good
name. It was obviously a space that had been designed to provide the best possible view of the dunes,
the beach, and Lake Michigan. This was the part of
the house Joe and I had seen from the lake, the part

that had seemed to hover over the dunes like a space-ship just about to land.

The area was about thirty feet deep, with glass walls forming a sort of eight-sided drum that stuck out from the house like a pavilion. Mrs. Schrader sat next to the farthest window. She was in her wheel-chair, and as Ms. VanTil and I entered the room she pivoted around to face us.

"Hello, Lee," she said. "Everyone always wants to see the overlook, so I thought I'd wait for you out here."

"It's spectacular," I said. "And you're right; I did want to get a look at it. I'd seen it from the lake, and I was curious about what all that glass enclosed."

Rachel Schrader turned her chair toward the lake again. "There's no point in a beach house, of course, unless you make the maximum use of the lake view. And I wanted to see the beach year-round, not just in the summer. I told the architect I didn't want one of those boxy enclosed decks that are the usual solution."

"He certainly took you at your word."

"Some people find the view of ice and snow and frigid water too chilling, but I enjoy it. Most of my family didn't agree with me. They like it in summer, when we open up the walls. Only Brad sees it the way I do. We think it's stimulating."

Before I could reply that it could definitely stimu-late an armful of goose bumps, Mrs. Schrader wheeled around toward me again. "But sit down, Lee. Hilda is bringing us some coffee. Unless you'd rather move back into the living room?"

"No. You're right. The view is lovely. And it's per-fectly warm out here."

The room held very little furniture, but I found a couch covered with brown sailcloth and sat on it. For twenty minutes Rachel Schrader and I chitchatted. We discussed the ecological problems of the Lake

Michigan dunes, but only in a general way. Nothing was said about the fact that my hostess owned a substantial stretch of those fragile dunes. Then she told me stories about my grandfather. She asked about my background, and I gave a short account of how I'd come to be born in Texas and how I had wandered back to Michigan two years earlier.

"Then you and Nettie are the last of the TenHuis family," Mrs. Schrader said.

"The last of our branch, I guess. Of course, Aunt Nettie's only a TenHuis by marriage. And I've never really been a TenHuis at all—by name or by culture. I know very little about the Dutch settlers of west Michigan and a lot about the cowboy culture of Texas. Warner Pier people have been kind, but I know I'll always be a stranger here in a lot of ways."

"I'm afraid that will always be true of Brad, as well. He didn't have an easy childhood. But he says Warner Pier is as close to a hometown as anywhere else, and I'm hoping he'll put down some roots. Which reminds me—Martin said you had had some computer problems."

I didn't quite understand what had reminded her of computer problems, but I didn't ask. "All of the Seventh Food Group have had problems. I'm afraid one of us passed a virus along to the whole group. But at the moment, we're all back up and running."

Rachel Schrader leaned forward, and her black eyes snapped. "Do you have any idea what happened?"

I was surprised at her interest. I know from Martin that Mrs. Schrader was in her late eighties. Lots of older people are into computers, of course, but it's usually because they need to use the gadgets for business reasons or for a hobby. I couldn't imagine that this was the case with Mrs. Schrader. I paused before I replied, trying to anticipate just how much information she wanted.

"I'm just a user, not a computer expert," I said finally. "But Warner Pier does have a computer guru, and he's working on the problem."

"He hasn't indicated exactly what virus is involved?"

She really was interested. I felt faintly surprised. "He hasn't told me anything, but my computer wasn't one of the ones with the major problem. I could ask him."

"Oh, no! It's just idle curiosity on my part. Schrader Labs has done research along this line, so I was curious. But I have no reason to bother anybody about it. It doesn't matter at all. Not at all."

Mrs. Schrader was certainly being emphatic about something that didn't matter "at all . . . at all." I tried to think of a tactful way to follow up on the subject. But my thoughts were interrupted by the sound of a door opening. Then a high tenor echoed through the house. "Grandmother! Where are you?"

Rachel Schrader did her pivoting act, turning toward the living room. "Out here, Brad!" Then her head snapped toward me. "I asked Brad to help load the boxes into your van."

Brad slouched into sight, coming through the living room door. He looked as hangdog as ever, as if somebody had just kicked him. Even the red plaid lumberjack shirt he wore didn't make him look cheerful. He kissed his grandmother on the cheek, then shook hands with me.

"Nice to see you again, Brad," I said.

"Oh, yes," he said. "We talked at Julie's memorial service."

I blinked, but I don't think I blew Brad's secret. He apparently didn't want his grandmother to know he'd come by my office to ask for advice on getting acquainted in Warner Pier. Just like he didn't want his uncle to know.

"Where are the boxes?" Brad said.

"Hilda will show them to you." Mrs. Schrader shook a misshapen finger at Brad. "This is your last chance, Brad. Are you sure you don't want any of Julie's dishes? At least you should take that good set of cookware. I know she'd want you to have it."

A look of complete revulsion flashed over Brad's face. For a moment I thought he was going to throw up.

Then he regained control. "No, thanks, Grand-mother. I'm saving my pennies so I can buy some-thing fancy. Until then I'll get by with my Kmart set." He grinned stiffly. "I'll just find Hilda. She'll show me the boxes."

"Now, Brad, don't run off the way you did last time," Mrs. Schrader said. "I want to talk to you."

Brad nodded and left. I got up as well. "I'll open the van, then help Brad," I said. "This is a very gen-erous gesture, Mrs. Schrader."

"When we get to Julie's furniture, I'll send it di-rectly to the shelter. And one other thing." Mrs. Schrader produced a checkbook from a purse that hung from the arm of her wheelchair. She flipped it open, found a white ballpoint pen in the purse. De-spite her warped fingers, she wrote rapidly.

After she'd ripped out the check, she folded it in half and held it out to me. "Here. This goes with the items." Then she smiled. "And take the pen, too. It's one of the new Schrader Labs promo pieces. They write quite well."

I wasn't so crass as to peek at the amount of the check, but I looked the pen over and gushed a bit. It was a nice one—the kind with gel ink—and had a tasteful design of a computer mouse chasing a lab mouse, spiraling around the body and down toward the writing end. Then I shook her hand—remembering to hold it gently—said good-bye, and went out the front door.

Brad was coming around the side of the house,

carrying a large carton. Hilda VanTil was with him with another carton. I opened the van. There weren't a lot of belongings being donated. Hilda and Brad each brought out one more box, and I carried one out. That was it.

I expected Brad to go back inside in obedience to his grandmother's instructions, but he stood there on the porch, not saying anything. It was left to the sweet-faced Ms. VanTil to give me a warm good-bye in her squeaky voice. She added directions for how to get off the property. The drive was one-way, she said. I was to go forward. In my rearview mirror I saw her entering the front door, and Brad heading around the side of the house.

The outbound section of asphalt drive led through the same sort of woods that the inbound road followed. The whole thing was well-plowed, but I drove slowly, enjoying the snowy woods. Frankly, as a person born on the Texas plains, I find the thick woods of Michigan's summer a bit scary. I like them a little better when the leaves are off the trees.

I was so intent on the scenery that when a figure in a red plaid jacket bounded out in front of the car, I nearly ran him down.

I threw on the brakes and luckily didn't hit an ice patch. The van came to a stop safely, and I rolled my window down.

"Brad! You nearly scared me to death!"

"I'm sorry. I was trying to catch you before you got out the front gate."

"How'd you get here?"

Brad gestured behind himself. "There's a bunch of paths and roads through the middle. I use them all the time. Looking at birds and such. But I wanted to tell you something about Julie."

"What about her?"

"The person she was really scared of was that guy with the ponytail. Jason."

Chapter 18

"Why? Why do you think Julie was scared of Jason?"

Brad shuffled his feet and looked more pitiful than usual. "It was all very nebulous."

"Come on, Brad! She must have said or done something to make you think she was afraid of him or you wouldn't say that she was."

"Well, once I was at her place, and the phone rang. She said, 'That might be Jason. I don't want to talk to him.' Then she let the answering machine pick up. And it *was* Jason. She made a face and turned down the volume so that she couldn't hear his voice. And I said, 'Who's Jason? A new boyfriend?' And she laughed, and she said, 'Not one of mine. He's a restaurant guy I know. He's pretty scary. He makes me feel creepy. I'm trying to avoid him.'"

"Did she say why she found Jason scary?"

Brad shook his head.

"That *is* pretty nebulous," I said. "Have you told the police this?"

Brad shook his head again. "They weren't very interested in talking to me."

"Why are you telling me?"

"You seem to know all those cops. Maybe you could drop a hint."

"I'd have to tell them it doesn't jibe with what I observed about Julie and Jason's relationship, Brad. They always acted like pals."

"I know it's screwy." Brad began to back away. "I've got to get back to Grandmother's house."

"Wait a minute, Brad. When did this episode happen?"

He was still edging away. "A couple of weeks before Julie . . ." His voice seemed to fail, and he turned. He called back over his shoulder as he ran back into the woods. "That's all she said!"

I watched him go. He slipped on the snow, but he didn't fall. He seemed to know just where to put his feet.

"That's the strangest thing Brad has done yet," I said aloud. "Running through the woods to tell me Julie said Jason made her feel creepy. That's impossible to believe."

I drove on, thinking furiously. Could Julie have been frightened of Jason? Saying he "made her feel creepy" didn't exactly prove that. Frankly, a lot of people are creeped out by openly gay guys with long gray ponytails, though I wouldn't have expected Julie to be one of them. Guys like that are very common in the Warner Pier area, since we're on the artsy side around here. Openly gay guys with long ponytails of any color fail to cause much excitement in our town, and Julie had always claimed that she especially loved Warner Pier.

Of course, Jason had admitted he was really angry with Julie after she "outed" him and Ross to Ross's elderly dad. Maybe that had happened about the time that Jason made the phone call Brad had overheard. But by the time Jason told me about the incident, he hadn't sounded as if he was furious with

Julie. He sounded exasperated at her naivete, but not as if he'd been ready to sever all ties with her. He hadn't resigned from the Seventh Food Group over it.

So, should I do anything about Brad's report? I could tell Hogan Jones. But what would be the point?

I still hadn't decided whether or not I should repeat Brad's story to Hogan Jones when I reached Warner Pier. That's when I noticed something unexpected—a car pulling into the parking lot at the Warner Pier Chamber of Commerce office.

But it was Sunday. The office should be closed. Then I remembered. The chamber's executive committee was driving up to Grand Rapids as a group that afternoon to attend a reception for the congressional delegation. Apparently I'd driven by just as the group began to gather.

On an impulse, I wheeled into the parking lot. If the chamber manager was there, I could hand in Mrs. Schrader's check immediately. I also might be able to pick up the key to the storage unit where the items collected for the women's shelter were to be stashed.

The chamber office is near the Interstate in a building that, in one of those small-town coincidences, once held my grandfather's service station. It had been remodeled until its origins were completely disguised, of course, and now featured shingled sides and cobblestone panels that made it look more like a summer cottage than an office. The canopy that once sheltered the gas pumps was gone.

I parked the van beside a big black sedan, almost large enough to be classified as a limo. On its door was a very tasteful logo, white with a few accents of red, featuring an abstract wing. The words "Eagle Heights Real Estate Development" were painted below in letters so modern and so small they were almost unreadable.

Eagle Heights was owned and operated by the vice president of the chamber, Barry Eagleton. I knew him, of course, since we both served on the chamber board of directors. But I'd never noticed this car before. It must be new, I thought. Very classy. But why did it seem so familiar?

I had climbed out of the van and waded through the slush to reach the entry to the chamber office before I remembered. Then I whirled around for another look at that eagle logo.

The day Martin Schrader and I had lunch at the Sidewalk Café, Martin had been late. And when he arrived, he got out of a big black Lincoln sedan with a black-and-white logo on the front door. I hadn't seen who was driving, but the logo had included a red wing, over lettering too small to be deciphered from inside the restaurant. Now I decided the car must have belonged to Eagle Heights Development. And Martin Schrader had told me he was in Warner Pier that day "for a business meeting."

I stared at the black sedan and thought. The easiest conclusion I could jump to was that Martin Schrader had been meeting with Barry Eagleton. In other words, the potential heir to one of the biggest pieces of undeveloped property in the Warner Pier area had been meeting with the biggest developer of property in the area. Was Martin looking into a deal for developing the Schrader property?

I got quite excited. Then I told myself to calm down. There were a dozen other explanations.

Maybe Barry hadn't been driving the sedan with the logo that day. Maybe it had been his sexy secretary. Of course, I didn't know that Barry had a sexy secretary, but if he did, Martin might have been riding around with her for reasons having nothing to do with real estate.

Or maybe Barry and Martin were looking into some sort of development deal that had nothing to do with the Schrader summer place. Martin or the Schrader family might well own other land in the Warner Pier area.

Or, maybe they were discussing some business deal that had nothing to do with development at all. Heck, maybe they were considering buying an aluminum storm door business. Or a health food shop. Or a car wash.

Maybe they'd known each other for years and had simply gone out for coffee. Or maybe Martin wanted to buy a house. Barry sold houses, as well as developing subdivisions.

But one thing was for certain. If Martin and Barry had been driving down Peach Street at noon, there was nothing secret about their meeting. Probably everybody else in town already knew about it.

So I could simply go inside the chamber office, talk to my fellow board member Barry Eagleton, and ask him what the heck he and Martin were up to.

I opened the door and went in. Several members of the executive committee were standing around and greeted me. I assured them I hadn't come to join the trip to Grand Rapids. Then I walked over to Zelda Gruppen, the chamber manager, who was sitting at her desk. Barry was standing near her.

Barry's a short guy—the top of his head is about even with my shoulder. He has slicked-down black hair, heavy eyebrows, a thick midsection, and a perpetual grin.

"Hey, Zelda. Hey, Barry." I remembered that Barry is one of the guys who kids me about my Texas accent, so I drawled the words out. Might as well let him have a laugh.

"Look what I've got." I waved Mrs. Schrader's check. "A donation to the drive to benefit the women's shelter. Isn't that as cute as a spotted pup under a red wagon?"

Then I told them where the check came from and gave a short version of how I happened to be the one Mrs. Schrader gave it to. Zelda—who's a typical west Michigan Dutch blond: sturdy and blue-eyed— took the check, and we all whistled at the amount.

"I've also got several boxes of clothes and household goods in the van," I said. "If you'll lend me the key to the storage shed, I'll take 'em over."

"Super," Zelda said. She took the key from the center drawer of her desk and handed it to me. "If we've left when you come back, just put the key in through the mail drop."

I turned to Barry. "Great car out there. Is it new?"

Barry's grin broadened. "Got it last week."

"It'll be awful nice for carryin' clichés—I mean, clients! Nice for taking folks around to look at property. A couple of hours in that dude, and they'll feel obligated to buy."

Barry chuckled. I wasn't sure if he was laughing at my twisted tongue or at the compliment to his car. "Keep 'em comfortable, I always say."

I leaned a little closer to him. "Say, did ah see you carryin' Martin Schrader down Peach Street a coupl'a days ago? What's he up to?"

Barry's grin became a bit forced-looking. "Oh, Martin's got lots of irons in the fire."

I smiled so widely I developed two new wrinkles at the corners of my eyes. "It's no secret that Mike Herrera is keeping a close eye on what the Schraders plan for their property south of town."

Barry looked away and rattled the keys in his pants pocket. "I guess the answer to that depends on just what happens when Rachel Schrader is gone."

"Martin didn't give you a hint?"

"Martin may not have much to say about the deal."

"Now, Brad, his nephew—he's such a tree hugger.

I guess he'd want the property to go to that ecology group he works with. Maybe Martin would go for that, too."

Barry shook his head slowly. "The Lake Michigan Conservation Society hasn't got any money to buy property. They expect it to be donated. I don't think Martin can afford to go that route."

Zelda jumped in then. "How can that be? Schrader Labs simply can't be in trouble. They just got a new government contract. There was a big story on the business page of the Grand Rapids paper last week."

"Schrader Labs ought to be in tiptop condition," Barry said. "But Martin doesn't own Schrader Labs. He's just a stockholder. His personal finances are another matter."

"Golly!" I said. "If he buys some chocolate, should I take a check?"

Barry laughed. "Oh, I'm sure his personal checks would be good. He's far from broke. You know how it is, Lee. Financial problems for the very rich are different from financial problems for people like you and me."

"I guess Martin's down to his last Mercedes," I said.

"Cadillac," Barry said. "He's a Michigan businessman, remember. We've all got to buy homegrown products."

We all laughed. I took the key to the storage shed and left.

So Martin might need money. Very interesting. Schrader Labs was in good shape, according to Barry, but Martin's personal finances needed a boost.

And the Schrader property at Warner Pier, or so Martin had said, was owned by his mother. There would be no financial benefit to Martin as long as she was living.

But so what? As Barry had said, financial problems for a person like Martin Schrader were different from the problems I might have. Where I might have to let my insurance drop if things got tight, a financial bind for Martin might mean he'd have to ski in Iron Mountain rather than Vail or cash in some stock he had intended to hold another year.

All this was interesting, but it didn't have any connection with my current problem. Should I believe Brad's tale about Julie being frightened of Jason? Should I report the yarn to Hogan? Should I call Brad and tell him I wasn't getting involved? Should I tell him to do his own dirty work?

I dropped the boxes for the women's shelter in their special storage unit, returned the key to the chamber office, and drove on to TenHuis Chocolade without reaching a conclusion. I went in, took my six breaths of chocolate aroma, and saw Dolly Jolly behind the counter. Seeing her there gave me an attack of conscience.

"Dolly, you're supposed to be learning how to handle chocolate, not working a cash register. I promise I'll stick around more."

"I don't mind, Lee!" Dolly's voice boomed as loudly as ever. "We've had hardly any customers! Guess they don't expect us to be open on Sunday. Nettie has me learning to tie those fancy bows! Packaging! That's part of the chocolate business, too!"

"Any messages?"

"Joe called!"

Joe answered at the first ring. The conversation didn't take long.

"Are you still planning to go to the preview of Jason's new place?" he said.

"I'd forgotten that was tonight. Do you want to go?"

"Since I'm almost the landlord, I guess it would be polite to show up."

"If you don't want to . . ." I knew going back to the house his ex-wife had built—where she and Joe had lived and where she had died—wasn't going to be easy for Joe.

"I can't let Warner Point become a hang-up. I want it to be a popular restaurant with loads of big dinners and receptions held there. So I'd better show. Lindy and Tony are going. And Mom and Mike will be there. Is seven o'clock okay?"

"Sounds great."

"Love you."

"Love you."

I hung up feeling a little warmer, despite the snow outside. It ought to be a pleasant evening. We don't see enough of Lindy and Tony. And I like Joe's mom. She doesn't hover, but she always seems concerned, unlike mine, who never seems to give a darn what I do. And Mike is good company, too, especially since he's almost quit trying to entice Tony into the restaurant business.

I really admire Mike, who worked himself up from a job as a dishwasher in Denton, Texas, to owning three restaurants and a catering service in a fancy Michigan resort. In fact, I often rely on Mike's advice, and now it occurred to me that he might help me solve the puzzle of what Brad had said about Julie being afraid of Jason. If anybody knew Jason, it was Mike. Jason had worked for him for years. Maybe Mike would know more about Jason and Julie's relationship than I did.

It was, I decided, worth a try. So I called Mike. I caught him at the Sidewalk Café. He agreed to drop by my office after his lunch rush was over.

He came in the door at two o'clock, looking a bit harassed, and plunked himself into the one chair in my little office. "What can I do for a fellow Texan?"

I'd decided to be deliberately vague. "I had it on good authority that a gal I know is afraid of Jason," I said. "But I've always thought he's a pussycat. Can you think of anything that might have caused that kind of a reaction to him?"

Mike rolled his eyes, and when he spoke his Tex-Mex accent suddenly appeared. "I thought that ol' affair had deesappeared. Won't people ever let nothin' be forgot?"

Chapter 19

I'm sure my jaw dropped, but it didn't take me too long to recover. "Okay, Mike. Spill it," I said. "There's no way for me to learn the local gossip but to ask. What are you talking about?"

"Eet was jus' a misunderstanding."

"Who misunderstood?"

"One of the waitresses." He rolled his eyes again. "She was new, and she didn' get it. Jason, he's a good-looking guy, and he doesn't act like he's . . ."

Words failed him, so I completed his sentence. "Jason doesn't swish, and the waitress didn't realize he's gay."

"Yes. She made eyes at him. I don't think Jason caught on. But she thought . . ." Mike's vocabulary failed him again.

"She thought he understood her overtures?"

"Yes. So she waited for him in the parking lot after closing—one thirty in the morning. When he went to his car, she tiptoed up behind him, and she . . ." He ran out of words again.

"She put her arms around him, or something like that. How did Jason react?" I chuckled.

Mike looked pained. "Eet wasn't funny! He was startled, you see. So he threw his elbow . . . she got pushed to the ground. She broke her arm."

"That's awful! I can see it wasn't funny at all."

"Jason called an ambulance. He tried to apologize. But . . . she was embarrassed. She filed charges."

"What happened?"

"I talked her into dropping them. The chief understood it was jus' an accident. Jason paid her doctor bills. She moved to South Haven. I helped her get a job down there."

"But it caused a lot of gossip."

Mike looked miserable. "I hoped the gossip had gone away. Who's telling it now?"

"Nobody really, Mike." I sighed. "Brad Schrader— you know, the cousin of Julie Singletree . . ." Mike nodded, and I went on. "Brad told me Julie was afraid of Jason. He said he didn't know why. I suppose Julie could have heard something about that incident. But I think the idea of her being afraid of Jason is nonsense."

"Jason and Julie worked together a lot. I thought they were friends."

"So did I. Jason introduced me to Julie. But Julie did find things out. She had an uncanny knack for picking up gossip. I guess she could have heard this story, or a garbled version of it, someplace."

"It's been five years. I hoped it had gone away. But I guess it never will. After Julie was killed, the Holland detectives hauled Jason in and questioned him a long time. I thought that was the reason." Mike got up. "I know you won't say anything, Lee."

I put my fingers to my lips and pantomimed turning a key. Then I changed the subject. "I'm looking forward to tonight."

"Yes, Jason's new restaurant is going to be very fancy, and we'll be the first to eat there."

I knew that Jason wanted his new restaurant, Warner Point, to be an elegant dining experience, so as soon as I got home I examined my closet for something elegant to wear to the opening. I nearly came up empty. My wardrobe was long on casual—khakis, jeans, sweaters, and T-shirts. Elegant was in short supply.

Finally I discovered a white silk shirt and put it on over my good black wool slacks. Then I remembered the big, cold, black-and-white main room in the Warner Point house, and I took the shirt off and put on a black cashmere turtleneck. It had been my Christmas present from Joe and I didn't get too many chances to wear it. But the solid black outfit made me look as tall and bony as Abraham Lincoln. So I put the white shirt on over the sweater—buttoned, but not tucked in. I dug through my limited stock of scarves and found a long, thin one striped in jewel tones and accented with gold thread. I draped it under the shirt's collar and tied a knot in each end. I put on my good leather boots.

That was as elegant as I could manage. At least Joe gave a low whistle when I came down the stairs.

Then he grinned broadly. "Jason's going to want you as a permanent hostess. You're going to fit right in."

"What do you mean?"

Joe's only answer was to shake his head, but when we walked into the main room of Warner Point, I saw exactly what he had meant. I matched the decor so closely it was almost funny.

The Warner Point house, built by famed defense attorney Clementine Ripley in consultation with a famous architect, had not appealed to me on the few occasions I'd visited it. The walls of the main living area were heavily textured and painted a stark white. The finish of the woodwork and floors was dark, almost black. The furniture had been either upholstered in white or else dark and spindly. The artwork had been practically nonexistent. There had been no window treatments—just walls of unadorned French doors. I had thought the room felt like an icebox, even in July. The idea of it in winter, with all that stark white and black, plus views of snow and ice out those French doors, had been bone-chilling.

But Jason had warmed it up. And he'd done it by using jewel tones.

The fireplace, for example, was made of blocks of white stone that were reminiscent of chunks of ice. It had no mantel, and the stone was piled right up the wall, clear to the high ceiling. Now, in the center of that expanse of stone was a wool tapestry in an abstract design and executed in brilliant colors. It hung like a banner above a cheerful fire.

The French doors now were hidden by draperies of deep red velvet. The round tables that had replaced the spindly wooden furniture were covered with stark white linen, true, but each had a centerpiece of a glowing candle surrounded by a heap of shiny metallic starbursts. Colorful paintings and hangings and more candles in wall sconces formed cheerful vignettes for the smaller tables that lined the walls.

But Jason had left the stark white walls and dark, almost black, woodwork and floors. So Joe had been right. My outfit fit right in. My black slacks matched the floors and woodwork, my white shirt matched the walls, and the jewel-toned scarf matched the decorations. I looked as if I worked there.

I exchanged an understanding look with Joe, and we both laughed. Then we greeted Jason, made obligatory—and sincere—sounds of admiration, and accepted glasses of champagne. We circulated.

The room was rapidly filling up. The whole Seventh Major Food Group had apparently been invited. Diane and Ronnie Denham were circling the hors d'oeuvres, both looking rosy and Santa-ish. Margaret Van Meter rushed over to give me a hug. As usual, her hair was straggly, and she wore a dress that was too tight, but her smile was so sweet it didn't matter. Jim was one of the few guys there without a tie, and both of them were obviously excited to be having a night out. Jim's parents were baby-sitting, Margaret said. Lindy and Tony weren't there yet, but I knew they were coming.

Most Warner Pier city officials had come, too. Mayor Mike was there, of course, escorting Joe's mom, Mercy Woodyard. I spotted the city clerk and all but one of the city council members, and members of the chamber's board were coming in, too. I knew Chief Jones had been invited, but Aunt Nettie had told me he was at a meeting in Lansing. She had declined an invitation to come with Joe and me, saying she wouldn't mind an early night.

The only person whose presence surprised me was Martin Schrader. He came in with Barry Eagleton. Which was interesting. Neither of them seemed to be talking business that night.

I was thinking that it was nice to have a purely social evening for a change, but that changed when Lindy came in.

She rushed in the front door and dashed across the foyer. She paused and scanned the room, obviously so excited that the beautiful surroundings were making little impression on her. When she saw me, she practically ran in my direction.

"Lee! Lee! I've remembered something!"

"What?"

She answered in a whisper that carried through the room more loudly than a shout would have. "That car that nearly pushed us off the road! It was an old Jeep!"

I took her by the arm and led her into a corner. Then I tried to speak in a whisper that *was* a whisper. "How did you decide that?"

"Tony and I came in my rental car, the one the

insurance company came up with, and I drove. A car came up behind us, and— Oh, Lee, those headlights looked exactly the same as the ones the other night. It had those up-and-down bars between them. Like long, horrible teeth. I nearly panicked."

"How did you find out it was an old Jeep?"

"It followed us into the parking lot here. It was Father Snyder."

"Father Snyder?" Father Snyder was the local Episcopal priest. "I can't imagine that he tried to push us off the road."

"Oh, I know that! I'm sure it wasn't him. But I do think it was somebody in an old Jeep like his. Come on! Father Snyder's waiting outside so you can take a look!"

Lindy dragged me outside without even letting me stop for my coat. Tony and Father Snyder were standing beside the priest's beat-up old Jeep. Both of them looked thoroughly ill at ease.

"Turn on the lights," Lindy said. "Let Lee see it."

Father Snyder, who's a round, cheerful young guy, spoke apologetically. "I like to drive this old rattle-trap in the snow. I let my wife have the good car— unless I need it for a funeral." He obediently climbed into his car and turned the headlights on.

"See!" Lindy was attracting a lot of attention from other people who were arriving. "See, Lee!"

I considered the front of the old Jeep. "Lindy. I didn't get as good a look as you did. I can't say one way or the other."

"Oh, Lee!"

"You were looking at the front of that car in your rearview mirror, Lindy. I looked back, but all I could see was bright lights and glare."

Lindy deflated like an inner tube at the end of a day at the beach. I patted her on the shoulder. "Listen, you need to tell Chief Jones about this. It might give him a valuable lead."

We settled for that. I led the way inside—I was freezing—and Lindy agreed to call the chief the next morning. Then I tried to remember how to have fun at a party.

It wasn't easy. Margaret and Jim didn't know many people, of course, so Lindy and I talked to them a lot, and we tried to introduce them around. Then Joe got cornered by one of the city councilmen, and I finally abandoned him and went looking for another glass of champagne. Jason was serving the sparkly, so he took the opportunity to introduce me to Ross, his partner. Ross seemed to be a nice guy, but as soon as Jason moved away, he began to quiz me about the current murder mystery. What had I thought of Julie? Why on earth would anyone have killed Carolyn? It's hard to be sociable when you're being cross-examined.

Finally, I simply muttered a lie—"I think my fiancé needs rescuing"—and went back to Joe. He did look happy to see me, and when I told him he needed to talk to his mother he seized the excuse and told the councilman he'd "research the question." We both fled toward Mercy.

Mercy was talking to someone who had his back to us. All I could see was a well-fitted, dark gray suit and a well-disciplined head of gray hair. Then he turned around, and I saw that it was Martin Schrader. Here I'd wanted to talk about something besides Julie's murder, and I had accidentally sought out the victim's uncle.

Mercy didn't seem sorry for us to interrupt her tête-à-tête with Martin. I was not surprised when she introduced him as a client of her insurance agency.

"Mercy saved our bacon two years ago, when the roof blew off the cabin," Martin said cheerfully. "She'd talked me into upping the coverage on contents, thank God. That stuff I thought was old furniture turned out to be antiques, and we got a nice settlement for water damage. We were able to refurnish the place."

"The cabin?" I said. "Is that the little house where Brad lives? Just as you enter the property?"

Martin looked at me sharply. "Yes, Brad lives in the cabin. He hasn't been bothering you, has he?"

"Oh, no." I belatedly remembered that I wasn't supposed to tattle on Brad and let his uncle know he had come by my office. "I like Brad. He helped me load up the things your mother gave to the chamber's campaign for the women's shelter."

Martin drained his glass, and I decided it hadn't been his first drink. Or his second or third. He turned his full attention on me. "Now what's the deal on this accident you and Mike Herrera's daughter-in-law had?"

I decided I didn't want to give Martin Schrader a full-scale description of the excitement. "Some guy tried to pass us there where the bank has fallen away on Lake Shore Drive," I said. "He got too close and shoved us over the side, but luckily we didn't go down where it's the stickiest. I mean, steepest! We missed the steepest part. Neither of us was hurt, but the driver left the scene."

"Where does Father Snyder's Jeep fit in?"

"I don't think it does." Martin frowned—maybe glared—and I felt that I had to go on. "Lindy saw Father Snyder's headlights in her rearview mirror tonight. She thinks the driver we tangoed with—I mean, tangled with! She thinks the driver who almost hit us may have driven an older Jeep like Father Snyder's."

"What do you think?"

"I didn't get that good a look at the car. Of course, Lindy's insurance company would like to find him. Her car was totaled."

I decided it was time to change the subject, even if it went back to Julie. "We—I'm speaking as a mem-

ber of the Warner Pier chamber's board—appreciated
the donation of Julie's household goods to our drive
for the women's shelter."

"That was Mother's idea. She knew Julie loved
Warner Pier."

"Were Julie and your mother close?"

"Mother was as close to Julie as anyone was, I
guess. Julie had kept her distance from most people
since . . ." He stopped talking, and I mentally finished his sentence with *since her husband turned out
to be such a louse.* I cast around desperately for another subject for conversation.

"Your mother seems very—well, strong. At least
mentally. I know she has trouble getting around."

"You're right; she's strong mentally. She's had several bad shocks in the past few years, and she rolled
with 'em better than I have."

"At least she still has you and Brad."

Martin's face grew bleak. "Yes, she has Brad."

"He certainly seems to be fond of her. And at least
he lives fairly near to her, though Warner Pier isn't
that close to Grand Rapids. He drives there to
work, right?"

"Yes." Martin gave me a sharp look, but he didn't
say anything more. Obviously he didn't like to talk
about Brad any more than Brad liked to talk about
him. I paused and tried to think of a different topic
to introduce. But Mercy jumped in before my tiny
brain could improvise.

"Brad came to me for car insurance," she said. "I
mentioned that so many people check out insurance
online now. I was surprised when he said he never
touches computers."

Martin looked at her sharply. "Why did that surprise you?"

Mercy smiled. "Because of his age, I guess. It
seems as if everybody under thirty-five is a computer
whiz these days."

"Oh, yes. Brad avoids computers. He's a regular computaphobe." Martin gave a barking laugh, then looked at his empty glass. "Guess I'd better get another drink," he said. He walked away, reeling only slightly.

I moved close to Mercy. "I hope Martin Schrader isn't driving," I said softly. "As his insurance agent . . ."

"I don't handle the Schrader cars," she said. "Just the Warner Pier property. It's a sort of a sop they throw to local business. But I'll put a bug in Barry's ear. Martin's definitely had enough."

She moved away, and Joe put his arm around my shoulder. "Let's go talk to somebody we really like to talk to," he said.

"How about Father Snyder? He's an awfully nice guy, and I don't want him to get the idea Lindy and I think he's the one who pushed us into the lake."

"Fine." Joe moved closer and spoke directly into my ear. "You sure are a knockout tonight. I could feel romantic, if I got a little encouragement."

I moved slightly closer to him. "Consider yourself encouraged."

He held my hand as we headed across the room, toward Father Snyder.

With the prospect of a romantic session with Joe to come, the rest of the evening went well. Joe and I helped each other dodge people—such as city council members—that one or the other of us didn't want to talk to. And if my spirits needed bucking up, I only had to catch Joe's eye. He'd always smile at me. He's a wonderful guy, I told myself. He loves me. A little thrill would travel up and down my innards. For the first time since Julie had been killed, I guess, I remembered how lucky I was.

The feeling didn't go away. It lasted through our good-byes to Jason, through a sort of preliminary courting session in Joe's truck, up the stairs to his apartment, and—well, clear through bacon, scrambled eggs, and coffee in his kitchen at four a.m. Joe didn't even bring up our wedding plans, bless his heart.

Crime only intruded again after I told Joe I had to go home.

He kissed me. "You're sure?"

"I've got to get some other clothes and my own car so I can go to work. Tomorrow's Monday."

"If you'd leave a few things over here . . ."

"It won't be long until I'll take over the closets and drawers, and you'll have to keep your stuff in a cardboard box."

He laughed. "I'll get some clothes on."

I began to gather up my belongings. My white silk shirt was draped over the back of the couch, but I had to look for a few minutes before I found the jewel-toned scarf. It was on top of my purse, heaped up in a chair—a regular nest of rich reds, blues, greens, and purples, shot with gold.

And in the middle of it was a white stick.

I stared at it a few seconds before I figured out what the white stick was. It was the white pen that Rachel Schrader had given me. It had fallen out of my purse and was lying among the folds of the colorful scarf.

It seemed familiar, somehow. But why?

I stared at it a long moment before I remembered.

The last time I'd seen Carolyn Rose, she'd had a bunch of colorful ballpoint pens fanned out in a brass jug on her desk. And in the middle of them had been one bright white pen.

Carolyn had picked it up and looked at it closely. Then a smile had spread over her face. A tricky smile, sort of sly-looking. She'd tucked the pen in her desk drawer.

The next day, Carolyn Rose had been dead.

Chapter 20

I was still thinking about that white pen Carolyn had pulled out of the jar of colored ones when I climbed into my own bed to catch a couple of hours of sleep before I had to get up and go to work.

I stared at the dark ceiling. Had the white pen been one of the Schrader ones? But Rachel Schrader had told me it was a new promotional item. She'd said I was getting one of the first ones given away. How would one have landed in Carolyn's pen jar?

Right after I'd left, Carolyn had apparently called Martin Schrader and left a message, asking him to drop by and talk to her. Could that have had anything to do with the pen? Could she have thought that Martin had left the pen? So what if he had? Although it didn't sound as if Martin had been around to see Carolyn for several years.

Unless . . . My half-waking mind went tripping back to the moment when Jack Ingersoll had urged Carolyn to look around for signs of a break-in. I had followed her back to the workroom, and she'd spotted the dirt in the sink. Had she picked up a pen from the counter then? I closed my eyes and concentrated. Yes, she had picked up a pen from the counter, then used it to point at the window catch.

Had that pen been white? I thought it had.

Could that have been the pen she later pulled from the jar on her desk? Could she have thought that pen had been dropped by the burglar? Could she have thought that burglar might have been Martin Schrader? Carolyn wouldn't have suspected Martin of killing his own niece, any more than I did. She might have called him to ask about the pen.

I turned over and whacked my pillow. It was too far-fetched. Impossible. The link between Martin Schrader and the white pen was simply too flimsy. Dozens of other companies distributed white pens as promotional items. Or you could buy a white pen that said something like "Bic" or "Rollerball" or "White Pen," for Pete's sake.

I guess I slept then, because the next thing I knew Aunt Nettie was moving around in the kitchen and it was seven a.m. But I was still thinking about that white pen after she'd left the house and I was eating my own breakfast. Finally, before I went to work, I called the Warner Pier police and got the department's secretary.

"Is Chief Jones still out of town?" I said.

"Until late tonight. Can I help you?"

"I suppose the chief did a complete listing of everything found out at House of Roses after Carolyn was killed."

"Complete? I'm sure he itemized everything connected with the crime."

"But not everything in the shop?"

"In a florist and gift shop? Like every rose, every vase, every piece of gift wrap, every little doodad House of Roses had for sale? We don't have that much paper in our budget, Lee. What did you have in mind?"

"It was a ballpoint pen." I could hear the indecision in my own voice. "I wondered, you know, if it might be a queue. I mean, a clue! It might be a clue."

There was a long silence before the dispatcher spoke again. "I don't know anything about a ballpoint pen. Jerry Cherry helped with the crime scene investigation. Do you want me to ask him to call you?"

"I guess so. It's obviously not an emergency."

It was nearly noon when Jerry called. I described the pen Carolyn had had and told him where I'd seen it.

"It wouldn't be on any kind of a list we'd keep," Jerry said, "an ordinary object like that. Unless it was found under the body or it was used as a weapon or something."

"Oh."

"But I've got the key. I could go out there and look for it. You say it was in a jug on Carolyn's desk, along with a bunch of those multicolored pens she handed out?"

"Right. But I think she put it in her center desk drawer."

I hadn't told him about my vague recollection that Carolyn had picked up a pen near the window the burglar had used. It simply seemed too silly. And I wasn't sure she'd done that.

Forty-five minutes later, Jerry called back. "No sign of the pen," he said. "It's not in that jug or in the center desk drawer. And I looked in the other desk drawers and by the cash register and other places where you might expect to find a pen. I didn't find it."

"That doesn't mean anything, does it? Some customer could have carried it away. Or Carolyn could have thrown it out."

"We did check the trash. It wasn't there. Listen, Lee, I'll tell the chief about this when he gets back. And Lindy called in this morning about the Jeep. I'll tell him about that, too."

Jerry and I chatted about Lindy's Jeep idea for a

few minutes, and I was careful to tell him that I couldn't identify the make of car.

"But Lindy feels certain that's what it was," I said.

Jerry Cherry wasn't the only person who heard about Lindy's identification of the Jeep as the car that had chased us. The Warner Pier grapevine had been busy. I had been getting phone calls from the minute I walked into my office. Barbara, my banker friend; some angry Episcopalian I had to assure that Father Snyder was above suspicion, even if he doesn't drive on snow very well; Diane Denham, who quizzed me about the Jeep, then mentioned that Jack Ingersoll had done a terrific job getting their computer back up. And on and on. I must have had a dozen calls about that darn Jeep that might not even exist.

It was around two when Brad Schrader wandered in. He looked unusually down in the mouth, and with Brad that meant he stumbled over his lower lip as he came in the door.

"You're probably busy," he said. "I can wait until you have time to talk to me."

I fought down the impulse to say I'd never have time to talk to him and motioned him toward a chair. "Come on in, Brad. What's up?"

He sat down. "What did you say to Uncle Martin last night? He put me through a big inquisition this morning."

Probably Martin's hangover talking, I thought. But it wouldn't be tactful to bring that up, so I made a noncommittal answer. "Your uncle quizzed *me* last night, actually," I said. "Whatever I said to him was in reply to a direct question."

"What was the deal about an old Jeep?"

"Probably nothing. Lindy thought the car that pushed us off Lake Shore Drive the other night might have been an older Jeep."

Brad looked at his shoes. "I guess that's why he

wanted to know if I'd been fooling around with the one in the storage shed."

I'm sure my jaw dropped. "There's a Jeep out at your grandmother's place?"

"It doesn't run. It's been on blocks since I was a kid."

"Where did it come from?"

"I think it was my grandfather's. He liked cars. He only used it to get around the property down here. Maybe he took it on camping trips with his buddies sometimes."

"So your uncle doesn't use it?"

Brad laughed scornfully. "Does Uncle Martin strike you as the type to go camping? He has nothing but contempt for nature!"

"Strictly a city boy, huh?"

"He can't tell a downy woodpecker from a hairy! Or a chickadee from a nuthatch! He thought phlox was a wildflower! The only stone he can spot is a Petoskey! The beach could wash out into Lake Michigan or be littered with medical waste, and he wouldn't even notice!"

Brad stopped talking and looked at me with an anguished face. "I'm sorry," he said. "I shouldn't have lost my temper. But Uncle Martin doesn't even care."

Wow. That had been quite an indictment. Somehow it made me like Brad better. When he had come out with that little tirade, he hadn't been self-conscious and only worried about himself. He really cared about the environment.

But his outburst explained one thing I hadn't understood. "I can tell you love living there in the woods," I said. "Even though it means you have to drive so far to work."

"What do you mean?"

"Don't you work in Grand Rapids? I guess I'm a

Texas chicken about the weather. I wouldn't want to drive ninety miles every day in the winter, though I know half the people in Warner Pier do. Of course, you have an ecologically friendly car."

"How did you know that?"

"A Prius was parked beside your house when I came out to see your grandmother. I assumed it was yours."

Brad nodded and stood up. "I've got to make that drive to Grand Rapids this afternoon," he said. "I'd better get on my way. I just wanted to warn you that Uncle Martin is on the warpath."

"I don't think he'll bother me, Brad. Don't leave without a sample chocolate."

Brad shook his head.

"Come on," I said. "Didn't you like the Jamaican rum truffle?"

Brad kept walking. "I'm sorry," he said. "I'm sorry." Then he was out the door.

I stared after him, mystified. "That whole family is nuts," I said aloud.

Why had Brad come in? To complain about Martin? I had nothing to do with Martin. Brad couldn't expect me to intercede between him and his uncle, could he? Intercede in what? I didn't understand why they didn't like each other, unless it was their differing ideas on the environment. If they had a quarrel, it was nothing to do with me.

But Brad's feelings about nature and the environment were rather touching. I made a mental note to check Aunt Nettie's bird book. I'd hate for Brad to find out I couldn't tell a downy woodpecker from a hairy, if that was his standard for judging environmental responsibility. And it wouldn't hurt to double-check which little black-headed bird was a chickadee and which a nuthatch. I knew both came to Aunt Nettie's feeder. I thought the chickadee was smaller and rounder.

Several customers came in during the next half-hour, so I spent quite a lot of time behind the counter. In fact, when the phone rang, I answered it out there.

"TenHuis Chocolade."

"Lee! Lee!" It was Lindy, and she was excited. "Have you looked at your e-mail?"

"No. I hope it's not gone again."

"Mine isn't, but, Lee, I can't believe it!"

"What? Calm down and make sense."

Her voice dropped to a dramatic whisper.

"Lee, I got an e-mail from Julie Singletree."

I nearly dropped the receiver. The shop whirled for a minute. Then I regained control of my voice. "If I ever got a message from the Great Beyond," I said, "I wouldn't expect it to come by e-mail."

"Well, you've got one. At least my message says it went to both of us."

"But it can't be from Julie."

"Oh, it's not! That's just the address it came from. It's from her grandmother. Go look at it! Quick!"

I called to Dolly Jolly, asking her to watch the counter. Then I picked up Lindy's call on my desk phone and commanded my computer to download the latest e-mail on TenHuis's second phone line. Sure enough, there was a message with the "partygirl" address that Julie had used.

"It does give me a funny feeling to see that," I told Lindy. "I wonder how Rachel Schrader got into Julie's e-mail."

"Read it!"

I opened the message. "Dear Ms. McKinney and Mrs. Herrera," it said. "I know you'll be startled to receive this message from me through Julie's e-mail. The truth is, something very surprising has come up, and I feel that the two of you can help me. I'm e-mailing because I don't want to take the chance of being overheard talking on the phone.

"I found Julie's Macintosh computer hidden here in my house. Only Martin would have had the opportunity to put it there. I simply do not understand what is going on, but perhaps the two of you could help me.

"Could you come out to the Warner Pier house for a short conference? I should arrive there by four thirty this afternoon.

"Needless to say, I would prefer that neither of you mentioned this matter to anyone else. I am determined to accomplish two things. First, to see justice done in Julie's death. There will be no cover-up. Second, I want to spare my family any unnecessary pain and notoriety. I'm sure you can understand my feelings.

"Martin has been called to a meeting in Detroit, and Brad will be working until late tonight. Only my faithful Hilda will be present. After we discuss the matter, perhaps the two of you will go to the police with me. It won't be easy for me to turn my son in to the police."

It was signed like an old-fashioned business letter. "Most sincerely, Rachel Schrader."

I read the letter twice. "That's crazy," I said.

"Lee, we can't refuse to go. Not when it's Rachel Schrader."

"Lindy, we don't know that this is from Rachel Schrader. It could be from the murderer. The police are assuming that he stole Julie's Macintosh."

"But if it *is* from her, Lee, it would be really rotten not to go and talk to her."

"I'm not going without checking it out."

"How are you going to do that?"

"I'll phone her."

"Where?"

"She gave me the numbers for both the Warner Pier house and her cell phone that time I had to go out and pick up Julie's stuff."

I spent ten minutes looking for the phone numbers.

This involved dumping out the gigantic tote bag I use as a purse and going through every scrap of paper and business card—and that was a lot of paper and cardboard. I finally found the numbers not in my purse, but scrawled on my calendar. I called the Warner Pier house, but there was no answer. Which was not surprising. Mrs. Schrader and Hilda VanTil were probably on their way down from Grand Rapids. So I tried the cell phone number.

"Hello!" Hilda VanTil answered with that distinctive high-pitched, nasal voice.

"Ms. VanTil? This is Lee McKinney."

"Oh, yes, Ms. McKinney. Mrs. Schrader said she had contacted you." Her voice faded as the cell phone displayed that common problem of cell phones along the lake shore. Then Ms. VanTil's voice came in strongly again. "You got her e-mail, eh?"

"Yes. I wondered . . ." I couldn't tell her I had wondered if the e-mail was really from Rachel Schrader. I improvised. "I was curlicue—I mean I was curious! Have you all left Grand Rapids?"

"Oh, yes! We just arrived at the Warner Pier house," she squeaked. "Mrs. Schrader is—well, indisposed. Can I have her call you back?"

"No. She wanted us to come out there. If she's arrived, Mrs. Herrera and I will be there shortly."

"Hokay! I'll tell her." Ms. VanTil's funny voice piped a good-bye.

This was beginning to sound as if it might be the real deal, though I still didn't understand just why Rachel Schrader would want to talk to Lindy and me before she went to the police. I called Lindy and told her as much.

"I don't see how we can refuse to go, Lee," she said. "It would mean denying a request from a grieving grandmother. And when that grieving grandmother is one of the wealthiest women in Michigan—well, just from a business standpoint, I feel we should go."

"Maybe so. But I'm getting legal advice first. I'm going to call Joe."

"But she said not to tell anybody."

"That's one of the things I think is the screwiest. Why doesn't she want us to tell anybody where we're going?"

Lindy said she'd come by to pick me up in her rental car. While I was waiting I called Joe. I got his answering machine at the boat shop, and his voice mail on his cell phone. I left messages describing the e-mail request from Rachel Schrader both places. Then I tried city hall. He wasn't usually there on a Monday, but he might have dropped by. He hadn't.

I gnawed my knuckles a minute, then called the police dispatcher. No, she couldn't get hold of Chief Jones, and Jerry Cherry was tied up with a three-car wreck down the street from the Superette. "Nobody's hurt," she said, "but he'll be over there for a while."

By then Lindy was in the shop, champing at the bit, ready to head out to the Schrader property. "I don't understand why you're dragging your heels," she said.

"After you've survived two attempts on your life, Lindy, I don't understand why you're so eager to go off to a lonely house in the woods." I sighed. "Let me tell Aunt Nettie that I'm leaving."

For once Aunt Nettie wasn't standing over a hot vat of chocolate. I found her in the break room. She has a desk there, though I've never known her to sit down at it and do any work. She uses it merely to stack papers and letters on. Anything private or important I file in my office, because once a paper hits Aunt Nettie's desk, it's lost until the odd moment when she loses something she really needs and decides to sort things out.

This happens maybe once a year, and this seemed to be the day. She had moved her pile of papers to one of the break room tables, and she was walking back and forth arranging things into stacks. I was pleased to see that she was also filling a black plastic trash bag.

I told her about Rachel Schrader's e-mail. "I've called her cell phone, and I talked to her assistant," I said. "I guess it's on the level."

Aunt Nettie frowned. "If you don't feel right about it, Lee, you shouldn't go."

"It's like Lindy says. How can we refuse a request from Rachel Schrader?"

"That reminds me." Aunt Nettie searched through one of the piles on the break room table. "I found this. It's that prayer for the working woman that Julie Singletree sent right before she died." She pulled out a stack of papers printed with Julie's distinctive rose background. "I read the poem, but I quit without reading the rest of the message."

"Julie's messages always had lots of junk at the bottom. Nobody ever read all of them. You can toss it out."

"Before you go, did you straighten out the Nordstrom order?"

We chatted about business matters for a minute. I reassured her about the Nordstrom order, and she explained a problem with an Easter bunny mold to me. Then I went around and gave her a hug before I left. "I shouldn't be too late," I said.

But I still felt uneasy, so when I got back to my office I ignored Lindy's pacing and insisted on one more check. I called the land line for the Schrader house.

"Hellooo!" It was Hilda VanTil again.

"It's Lee McKinney," I said. "We got held up, but we're on our way."

"I hope so. Mrs. Schrader is getting impatient."

Lindy was, too. I couldn't put her off any longer. We got into her rental car and headed out Lake Shore Drive. It was almost dark.

CHOCOLATE CHAT

CHOCOLATE AND ROMANCE

". . . The taste of chocolate is a sensual pleasure in itself, existing in the same world as sex. . . . For myself, I can enjoy the wicked pleasure of chocolate . . . entirely by myself. Furtiveness makes it better."

—Dr. Ruth Westheimer

" 'Twill make old women young and fresh;
Create new motions of the flesh.
And cause them long for you know what,
If they but taste of chocolate."

—James Wadworth (1768–1844)

(Description of lovelorn nobleman in seventeenth-century France) "His love for her was such that he shut himself in his room for months on end . . . without eating, drinking barely enough cups of chocolate to sustain him."

—Primi Visconti, quoted by Sophie D. Coe and Michael D. Coe in *The True History of Chocolate*

"It's not that chocolates are a substitute for love. Love is a substitute for chocolate. Chocolate is, let's face it, far more reliable that a man."

—Miranda Ingram

Chapter 21

L indy was excited as we drove along through the gathering gloom. She seemed to be anticipating an adventure. But I was glum. I still felt nervous about being asked to meet Rachel Schrader.

I guess it was nerves that made me turn around to see if there was a car behind us. There was, but it was turning left. It didn't look threatening.

I guess I'd reminded Lindy of our brush with death, because she spoke. "I don't think anybody is following us."

"It'll be a long time before I stop checking to see who's behind me."

"Me, too." Then she turned her compact rental car toward West Street, rather than toward the Orchard Street Bridge. "Let's go the long way around," she said. "I'm not all that excited about driving past that drop-off on Lake Shore Drive."

"Fine with me." I faced forward again, and in the process I somehow dumped my big leather satchel onto the floor. All my belongings landed under my feet.

"Dad gum! I just had everything out of that bag

earlier this afternoon," I said. "Don't make any sudden stops while I gather it all up."

"I'll have to slow down when I get on the Interstate."

I began to pick my stuff up and stow it back in the tote bag. It's not easy for a six-foot person to pick things up off the floor of a Neon, but I pushed the seat all the way back and tried. Sunglasses, billfold, keys—that was just the start. I carried far too much junk around with me. There was even a big sheaf of papers.

"I thought I got rid of all these papers back at the office," I said.

I picked the papers up and realized I was holding the printout of the long message from Julie, the one Aunt Nettie had had on her desk. It was the message that had caused me to request that Julie leave me off the list for inspirational items.

"I thought I tossed this into Aunt Nettie's trash," I said. The big print size Julie had used to send e-mail made the thing easy to read, even in a dim light. I thumbed though the pages as we drove. "Julie never killed anything," I said. "Here's that recipe for cookies Diane Denham sent out way before Christmas."

"How about the punch recipe that Carolyn sent? I meant to print that one out."

I looked further. "Looks as if it's not here," I said. The car swerved, and I looked up. Lindy was turning into the Schrader property.

"I guess that's Brad's house," Lindy said.

"Yes, just follow the road on around to the right. It makes a circle, and the main house is at the opposite end of the loop, on the lake shore." I looked back at the papers in my lap. "I'm pretty sure the punch recipe isn't here, Lindy. I'm down to the last page and it's . . ." My voice trailed off as I read what was on the last page. As I took it in, I began to feel almost dizzy with surprise.

Then Lindy threw on the brakes, and I almost hit the windshield.

"Lee!" She screamed my name. "Look!"

The car was completely stopped. Ahead of us, parked beside the road and plainly visible in our headlights, was an old, ragtop Jeep.

"Lindy!" I was screaming, too. "Drive on! It's too narrow to turn around and go back! Brad put that Jeep there as a trap! He wants us to get out and investigate! He's the murderer! Drive like hell!"

Lindy may have paused a second, but she didn't argue. She floored the Neon's accelerator, and the little car leaped forward. I craned my neck around, and I saw a figure run out of the woods, toward the Jeep.

Lindy yelled. "Are you sure that was a trap? What about Mrs. Schrader?"

"She's not here! That e-mail was a trap, too! And Brad must have imitated Ms. VanTil's voice when I called."

"How do you know?"

"It's in this e-mail. Brad told Julie what he was up to. He's planning to kill Martin! Julie thought he was kidding."

Ahead, the bulk of the flying saucer mansion became visible. As we reached the turnaround area in front of it, I yelled. "Stop!"

"What now?" Lindy hit the brakes and the Neon skidded to a halt.

"Listen," I said, "there's a road that cuts through the middle of the big circle drive. If we go on, Brad can cut us off. He's got us trapped if we go forward."

"What should we do?"

I took a deep breath. "Cut your lights."

Lindy complied. "Okay," I said, "I'm going to get

out. You turn the car around facing the way we came in. Can you do it without lights?"

"Sure. What are you going to do?"

"Break a window."

I didn't stop to explain. I jumped out of the car and headed for the flowerbed. I knelt and dug through the snow until I got hold of one of the ostrich-egg-sized beach stones that filled it. Then I staggered up the broad stairs, and hurled the rock at the window on the right side of the door. Nothing happened, except that the stone bounced back and nearly hit my foot. I picked it up and threw it again, tossing it as hard as I could.

This time the security system activated an alarm, and a deafening clanging noise began. I ran back down the steps, circled the car, and jumped in. Lindy's mouth was hanging open, but when I pointed forward she took off. There was just enough light to see the road without headlights.

I was terrified. Would my trick work? Had Brad taken the shortcut across the circle drive? Would he hear the alarm and think we'd tried to get into the house? Would he go there, looking for us? Or was he waiting for us right where we'd seen the Jeep, ready to ram into us?

Lindy was speaking, but I still couldn't hear a word. She didn't hurry; it was simply too dark. But she drove on steadily. Soon I saw the roof of Brad's cabin, a straight line against the twisted tree limbs.

The siren was far enough away now that I could yell and be heard. "Get out onto Lake Shore Drive. If Brad's waiting for us at the entrance, it's too late anyway! Then head for Aunt Nettie's."

Lindy flipped on her lights. "Okay, Lee," she said. "But you'd better be right about all this, or we're in a lot of trouble for breaking Mrs. Schrader's window."

I pulled the e-mail printout from behind me—I'd wound up sitting on it after I jumped back in the car—and tapped it. "It's all in here! As good as a confession. I've got to get this to Chief Jones."

Lindy wheeled onto Lake Shore Drive and floored the Neon. A blue truck loomed up, coming toward us. Its horn blasted, but we didn't stop.

Maybe we were in the clear. But no, behind us I saw lights bouncing off the trees, and a car turned into the road. Again the pickup's horn blasted, but the lights careened around the truck and came speeding toward us.

Lindy saw the lights. "Oh, god! It's the same lights I saw the other night!"

"He's not two blocks behind us." That meant we couldn't take the evasive action we had before, such as turning into a drive and hiding behind a hedge. If there had been a hedge anywhere.

Neither of us spoke. The Neon wasn't a fast car. But the Jeep was old. Could we outrun Brad? Could we get to Aunt Nettie's before he caught up with us? Was he armed? If we got to Aunt Nettie's would he shoot the place up?

I tried to think logically. Brad hadn't used a gun on Carolyn, and he hadn't used one when he chased Lindy and me. He'd killed Julie with his bare hands. He was into ecology, not hunting. The chance of his having a gun didn't seem large.

"We're going to have to pass that drop-off." Lindy muttered the words, but I knew what she said. I'd been thinking about the drop-off, too.

"We're going the other direction. He can't shove us toward the drop-off unless he gets on the right-hand side of the road."

Lindy's chin was grim. Her lips barely moved, but I heard her. "Damn it! He's not going to push us off this time!"

But as we got near the place where the bank had been eaten away, I realized that the Jeep was going to try just that. He pulled up close behind us, then swung right, as if he was going to pull around on our right-hand side.

"No, you don't!" Lindy yelled. She edged the Neon closer to the edge of the road, resisting the natural impulse to pull to the left and move away from the Jeep. The Jeep bumped our rear end, but Lindy squeezed a few more miles per hour out of the Neon, and we stayed on the road. The Jeep fell back, but I knew he would try again.

It was a nightmare—not only because we knew we were close to death, but because of the lighting. Our headlights were hitting the road ahead, and the Jeep's headlights were stabbing into the Neon's rear window with a harsh, brilliant light. It gave the whole chase a nightmare quality, as if it weren't really happening.

And then I realized that there was another set of headlights involved. They were high and bright, and they were behind the Jeep. A third vehicle was in the race.

I saw the Jeep shudder and veer across the road. But it hadn't hit us. What had happened?

It shuddered again.

"It's that truck!" I yelled it out. "It's behind the Jeep! It's bumping the Jeep the way the Jeep bumped us."

"That's *his* problem!" Lindy's voice was grim. She looked straight ahead, her hands gripping the steering wheel as if it were a life preserver and she had been tossed off a boat in the middle of Lake Michigan.

I watched out the back window. The Jeep shuddered again. It jumped ahead and nearly hit us. But the Jeep's driver—I was sure it was Brad—was worried about the truck behind him. Brad was weaving back and forth across the narrow blacktop.

Then it happened. The Jeep driver must have

thrown his brakes on. The old car veered across the road.

Then the Jeep hit a patch of ice. It spun around like an out-of-control merry-go-round.

The Jeep went through the orange tape alongside the washed-out area, clipped the edge of one of the concrete barriers, and plunged over the edge and down to Lake Michigan without ever slowing down.

Chapter 22

I yelled, "He's gone over!"

Lindy slammed on the brakes and pulled the Neon to the edge of the road, almost ramming its nose into a bank of piled-up snow. The truck stopped behind us. Its driver jumped out. Lindy jumped out. I crawled out, since I had to go out the driver's side because my door was jammed shut by snow. But it was only seconds before the three of us were in a group hug.

The driver of the truck, of course, was Joe. I think I was crying. I hope I told him how glad I was to see him.

The three of us ran back down the road to the spot where Brad had gone over. We could see the lights of the Jeep at the foot of the bank.

"I'll go down," Joe said. His voice was grim. "I already called the cops on my cell phone, and I've got a good flashlight in the truck."

"I can come, too," I said.

"I'll yell if I need help, Lee. Wait and wave the cops down when they get here."

Lindy moved the Neon so that its headlights gave

a little illumination to the area, and I used my cell phone to call the dispatcher, telling her we needed an ambulance, as well as law enforcement. Joe didn't come back up until the police were there. "It was Brad Schrader," he said. "Just the way you thought. He was thrown out halfway down. I don't think the EMTs will be able to help him."

Joe put an arm around both Lindy and me, and we stood at the top of the bank, looking down. "Maybe it's all for the best," I said. "Poor Mrs. Schrader."

"But why?" Lindy said. "Why would Brad try to kill us?"

"Because he killed Julie, Lindy," I said. "And he must have killed Carolyn, too."

"But why were we next on the list? We didn't know that."

"I think you did, Lindy. While we were standing around here, I remembered something. You went by Julie's the night she was killed."

"But I didn't see anything."

"You said there was a car—you called it 'a bug-eyed car'—in Julie's parking lot, right? You said you stumbled and fell into it."

"Yes, but—Lee, you know me. Unless the car was some odd color, I wouldn't know it again."

"But you also said it was parked backward."

"Right. It had been backed into its slot."

"It only just now occurred to me, but Brad parked his car backward in the shed out beside his house. And he drove a Prius, which is a rather unusual car. If he was inside Julie's apartment . . . if he looked out and saw you stumble and fall into his car . . . he'd find it hard to believe that you wouldn't remember it. And maybe you would have, eventually."

Warner Pier and Michigan State police were gathering, and Joe got permission for us to leave. The Neon and Joe's pickup had to stay there for the moment, so Aunt Nettie came to get us. It was at her house that the others read the message from Brad to Julie, the message I'd read in the car, the message I believed had caused her death.

It was far at the bottom of the long list of e-mails I had printed out and given to Aunt Nettie. I hadn't read it until that afternoon, and I'm sure none of the other members of the Seventh Major Food Group had read it either.

"Julie," it read. "Last night Uncle Martin admitted to me that he intends to develop the Warner Pier property as a resort. I could kill him! That land absolutely must be saved! The only hope is to give it to the Lake Michigan Conservation Society."

Brad and Julie had exchanged several other messages on the topic. Julie had tried to calm Brad down. But he had been adamant. "A louse who would treat the lake this way isn't even fit to live," Brad had written. "And Grandmother won't DO ANYTHING." He had put the words in all caps, the e-mail equivalent of shouting.

Julie, bless her heart, had replied with some stupid poem about good coming out of evil. She had later forwarded the same poem to the Seventh Food Group, with Brad's irate messages trailing along at the end.

Hogan Jones, who'd been informed about Brad's crash on his way back from Lansing, came by the house as soon as he could. Hogan read the printout and shook his head. "Sounds like Martin might have been meant to be the real victim. Brad obviously killed Julie, but I doubt it was premeditated. Julie just got in the way, sent this message on. He probably got mad about that and hit her."

"She was such a little thing," I said.

Hogan nodded solemnly. "Yes, Brad probably panicked when he discovered he'd killed her. And then

Carolyn Rose, Lindy, and Lee stumbled into the mess."

It was right at that moment that a car pulled into Aunt Nettie's drive. It crawled up to the house, paused, then inched into the parking area behind the house.

"Who can that be?" Aunt Nettie said.

"More cops?" I looked out the window. "Oh, golly! It's a big white Cadillac, and I think Rachel Schrader is in it!"

I was already feeling sorry for Mrs. Schrader, and as I watched Martin help her out of the car, I felt terrible. We all ran out to greet them, of course. We were all talking at once, offering to help with the wheelchair, to carry Mrs. Schrader, to do anything she needed done.

But she waved us aside. "I can walk as far as Mrs. TenHuis's door," she said. "It's only vanity that makes me use the chair."

She crept down the walk, leaning on Martin's arm, and I saw what she meant. Her limp was pronounced and unattractive. But she made it into the house. There she sank into a rocking chair and turned to me and Lindy.

"I've come to ask you young women to forgive me. To forgive Martin. If we'd acted on our suspicions you wouldn't have had this terrible experience."

I didn't know what to say, but Aunt Nettie saved the day. "Oh, Mrs. Schrader," she said. "It must have been awful to suspect your own grandson. No one can blame you for believing in him as long as you could."

Martin sank into a chair, his face gray. "Brad has nearly driven Mother crazy, ever since his parents died." He looked up at Hogan. "I guess you found out about the trouble he got into over hacking."

Hogan nodded, but I was mystified. "I thought Brad never touched computers," I said. I held up the computer printout. "I was surprised when I saw these messages to Julie."

Martin looked at his feet. "Brad was forbidden to touch a computer as part of his plea agreement," he said. "He was involved in the Ecoterror case. It took a lot of lawyers, but in the end the prosecutors couldn't prove that he'd actually been one of the hackers Ecoterror used, and he agreed to a plea bargain that avoided jail time. We had a hard time finding him a job that didn't involve computers. That's how he wound up in public relations. He only had to use a computer as—well, a typewriter. And he could be imaginative. He came up with the design for that new white pen.

"Mother and I have been frantic since Julie died. We knew Brad had a bad record, but we couldn't figure out any reason he would have killed Julie! He was closer to her than he was to anybody else. I kept telling myself I must be wrong, that Julie must have been killed by a burglar. Or a stalker."

He turned to me. "That's why I quizzed you, Lee. I hoped Julie had mentioned some threat. An odd phone call. Something."

Mrs. Schrader spoke. "And I had much the same idea, Lee. When I heard that your e-mail group had been hit by a computer virus of course I suspected Brad. But I couldn't understand why he would do such a thing. If he'd been caught, it would have meant prison."

I didn't say anything. Brad had gone far beyond sending a computer virus to the Seventh Food Group. He'd burglarized House of Roses, he'd knocked Lindy out and stolen her laptop, and apparently he'd even managed to get into my computer while he was waiting in my office.

Martin went on. "I kept hoping that Brad wasn't

involved until today, when I took a look at the old Jeep. Brad had put it back up on blocks, but a look under the hood convinced me he'd juiced it up so that it would run. I headed back to Grand Rapids to talk to Mother. I thought we could get a lawyer, then convince Brad he had to give himself up. But I was too late. Brad made one more attempt at getting you and Mrs. Herrera out of the way. Thank God you escaped!"

"Thank God Joe listened to his answering machine," I said.

"Thank God Lee was suspicious about the e-mail from Mrs. Schrader," Lindy said.

"But I called to check on that," I said. "Brad must have answered the phone imitating Ms. VanTil's voice. He fooled me completely."

"I'm sorry to say that the young people have made fun of poor Hilda's odd voice for years," Mrs. Schrader said. "Brad was particularly good at imitating her, because his own voice had a rather whiny sound."

Until then Mrs. Schrader had displayed an iron control, but now tears began to fill her eyes. "I'll always blame myself. I didn't get along with Brad's father. As a result, I didn't see much of either Brad or my son while Brad was small. I didn't realize what an unstable person Brad's mother was. I didn't step in when Brad was young; I did nothing to help a bad situation."

"Mother! Anything you had suggested would only have been seen as interference!" Martin shook his head. "Without his parents' cooperation, I don't think anyone could have helped Brad."

"I could have done more after they died, Martin. When Brad moved back here, I shouldn't have let him move out to the cabin. He was alone too much. He sulked and felt sorry for himself. And he got back into computers, despite agreeing not to do that. We should have done something to take him out of himself. I failed him."

"Julie tried to help him," Martin said. That comment seemed to end the discussion.

Brad's house was searched that night, of course, and we found out later that the final evidence turned up there. Julie's Macintosh computer and Lindy's laptop were hidden in a closet, along with a laptop that Brad apparently owned himself. Brad, of course, had never kept his agreement not to touch a computer.

Since Julie died, he'd been hooking into all the Seventh Food Group e-mails. Stupidly, none of us had taken Julie's address off the master list, so anything we sent to each other had gone to her address as well. And like most of us Julie kept her e-mail access code stored in her computer, so getting into her messages was no problem.

Brad had used Julie's e-mail when he pretended to be his grandmother and enticed Lindy and me out to the Schrader estate. If I hadn't disobeyed instructions and left a message for Joe, telling him where we were going, Brad might have trapped us. Joe had saved our lives.

No one understood exactly how Carolyn Rose got into the deal, but her phone record did show a call to the Schrader house in Warner Pier. As Joe and I pieced it together, she must have realized that someone from Schrader Labs had dropped the white ballpoint in her shop, and that—because she found the pen near the window the burglar had used—that someone had been involved in the break-in. She must have called Martin at Schrader Labs to tell him about it. Was she hoping to reestablish her connection with Martin? Maybe.

Carolyn left a message with Martin's secretary, but she then called the Schrader house at Warner Pier. Brad must have answered the phone. Carolyn would have had no idea that the white pens were a new item that only a few people had access to, so she probably mentioned the pen. Whatever she said to Brad, it caused him to come to her shop and kill her.

But Brad wasn't entirely cruel, I guess. The searchers also found a cage of pet mice in his house. There was a brown one, which Martin Schrader identified as Brad's. But there was also a white one which Martin identified as the mouse taken from Julie's apartment. All we could figure was that Brad hadn't wanted to leave it there unfed. That was the best we could discover to say about Brad.

One of the things that really mystified me was, why had Julie been afraid of Jason? It took me a day to realize that she hadn't been afraid of him at all. Brad had merely claimed she was, possibly trying to keep the police interested in Jason. He lied.

That night I felt truly sorry for both Martin and Rachel Schrader. I took a little comfort from seeing the tender way Martin handed his mother into her car. Now that she had only Martin to turn to, maybe they could comfort each other.

The Schraders had barely left when another car came up Aunt Nettie's drive. It was a compact car, not a law enforcement vehicle.

"Who can that be?" Aunt Nettie said.

The compact pulled around the house and stopped. A short, round guy—wearing a down jacket that made him look even shorter and rounder—got out.

Aunt Nettie gasped and ran out the back door. "Bobby! We've had so much excitement I nearly forgot you were coming!"

Bob came in rather nervously, as if uncertain of his welcome, but when he saw that Aunt Nettie was really glad to see him, he agreed to stay overnight, rather than driving three or four hours back to the Detroit area in the dark.

Bobby turned out to be well-scrubbed, with the square Dutch face so typical of Michigan. Once out of his down jacket, he wasn't as round or short as he'd looked getting out of his car. He was just a couple of inches shorter than I am.

Of course, he had to be introduced to Joe and to hear all about our excitement, so it was after ten o'clock and we were all eating pizza before he and Aunt Nettie began to talk about his job prospects.

"Did you bring us a résumé?" Aunt Nettie asked.

"No, I didn't," Bob said. "I appreciate your asking for one, but I'd really rather stay in the Detroit area."

I admit that I felt a weight lift from my shoulders.

Bob grinned in a way that looked a little like Aunt Nettie. "See, my girlfriend has another year in college. So, even if I don't find a real good job right away, I want to stay over there for now. I think maybe my girl—Lisa—is one reason Mom is pushing me to ask you for a job. She likes Lisa okay, but she thinks we're too young to settle down."

"Mothers are like that," Aunt Nettie said. "And she's got a point. You don't want to make lifetime commitments too early."

Bob nodded. "Oh, we're not rushing into anything. Besides—well, I've always worked in food service. I'd like to try something else, if I can."

Aunt Nettie smiled. "That makes sense, Bobby."

"Plus, I'm not sure I want to get involved with family—I mean in a business way. I want to—you know—prove I don't need to get any special treatment from relatives. Prove that I can make it in the real world."

Aunt Nettie looked at me. "Is TenHuis Chocolade part of the real world, Lee?"

I laughed. "It is during the weeks before Valentine's Day. The chocolate business doesn't get any more real than that. But Bob has a good point. Chocolate is a very specialized business. I can understand his wanting more general experience in a first job out of college."

Bob looked apologetic. "It's not that family isn't important, Aunt Nettie. It's just that I don't want to be too tied up with family. Unless it's with Lisa."

I thought about what Bob had said as I finished my pizza. Bob didn't want to be "too tied up" with family, except with his girlfriend, whom he obviously saw as his future wife.

I felt the same way about Joe. When I thought of family, he was the most important person who came to mind.

But there was more to it than that. Look at the Schraders. Mrs. Schrader hadn't gotten along with Brad's father. So she'd seen very little of Brad while he was growing up. Now she blamed herself for not making more of an effort to help him.

Maybe it wouldn't have made any difference. On the other hand, fifteen years earlier Aunt Nettie had taken in a difficult teenaged niece for the summer. Her kindness had laid the basis for a lifelong friendship between us. Plus, the example of a good marriage I'd seen as I lived in the same house with her and Uncle Phil—well, it had sure given me a better pattern than the one I'd gotten from my parents.

But my parents were still my parents, I realized, even if I got impatient with them. If one of them was sick, I'd be on the next plane to Texas. But what would we have to talk about after I got there? We'd grown so far apart. . . .

Before Joe left that night, I took him in the kitchen for a private talk.

"You're right," I said. "We do need to have a real wedding."

Joe looked amazed. Then he gave me a bear hug. And a big kiss. Then he spoke. "Wow! I'd given up on that. What brought about this change of heart?"

"Oh, I was thinking about how Mrs. Schrader regrets not making peace with Brad's father. I don't want to have that kind of regret when my parents are gone. Having them at the wedding won't be easy! They may refuse to come. But at least I can invite both of them. And Annie. And Brenda. But I think we should hold the wedding up here. Not in Texas. I'll gather my courage and do this, but I want them on my turf. Not me on theirs."

I agreed to call my dad the next day and to talk to my mother as soon as she came back from her current trip. Then Joe and I made a date to talk about all the details the next evening.

Then he went home. His truck had been released by the police, so I walked him out to it. I even sat in it with him for a while.

All the best stories end with a clinch.

CHOCOLATE CHAT

REFRIGERATOR MAGNET CHOCOLATE

"Hand over the chocolate and nobody gets hurt."

"Save the Earth. It's the only planet with chocolate."

"If there is no God, who created chocolate?"

"Money talks. Chocolate sings."[1]

"The four essential elements: Means, Motive, Opportunity and Chocolate!"[2]

1. Contributed by Nancy Lebovitz
2. © Instant Attitudes

JoAnna Carl
The Chocoholic Mystery Series

**EACH BOOK INCLUDES YUMMY
CHOCOLATE TRIVIA!**

Looking for a fresh start, divorcée Lee McKinney
moves back to Michigan to work for her aunt's
chocolate business—and finds that her new job
offers plenty of murderous treats.

The Chocolate Cat Caper
The Chocolate Bear Burglary
The Chocolate Frog Frame-Up
The Chocolate Puppy Puzzle
The Chocolate Mouse Trap
The Chocolate Jewel Case
The Chocolate Snowman Murders
The Chocolate Cupid Killings
The Chocolate Pirate Plot

OM00

P.O. 0005504351 202